RITUAL OF THE ANCIENTS

ROAN ROSSER

Rainbow Dog

RAINBOW DOG BOOKS

Your free ebook is waiting

Sign up for my newsletter to get Jack's prequel story for free. Available at https://bit.ly/3J1twim

CONTENTS

CHAPTER 1

DELICIOUS NEIGHBORS

THE LOCKED DOOR TO my apartment building stared at me mockingly. I rattled the door in frustration, then rested my forehead against the glass.

This was the capstone to a truly terrible evening.

"Fuck," I muttered to myself, but my words came out at less than a hoarse whisper. I coughed and massaged my neck, trying to clear my throat so I could buzz my roommate and ask her to let me in.

I hated to do it, given it was the middle of the night. Sleep deprived Lindsay was scary. But, as much as I dreaded her inevitable lecture on responsibility, I'd been mugged on my way home from work and the thief had made off with my keys—and almost everything else, including my museum employee badge.

At least, I assumed that's what had happened, since I had no memory of the time between leaving work and waking up in a dumpster covered in blood. I didn't even know whose blood it was, since I was unharmed except for a pounding headache and a sore throat. But it didn't really matter.

The important thing, the thing that would save this awful day, was that the mugger hadn't found the hidden pocket in my jacket that contained the golden amulet that I'd stolen as I left work.

With it in hand, I could finally pay off my debt to the mobsters. And maybe even have enough left over for top surgery. Everything else could be replaced.

However, this also meant I couldn't exactly walk over to the police station to report the mugging, and instead had to trudge home on foot, head pounding with each step. I probably had a concussion.

Steeling myself for Lindsay's yelling, I entered our apartment number into the keypad. The phone rang for a long time before Lindsay's voicemail picked up. She had probably turned off her phone. Not the first time I hadn't been able to reach her late at night.

I rattled the door again and then kicked it. I was exhausted and thirsty. So thirsty. All I wanted to do was drink a gallon of water and then crawl into bed.

I lingered by the front door while I debated what to do. If I got lucky, someone would come by and I could just follow them inside. But given it was the middle of the night, if I got unlucky I'd have to sleep outside.

I caught sight of my reflection in the glass and was horrified by the sight that greeted me. Nobody was going to believe I lived here looking like this. I scrubbed the worst of the dumpster's grime from my face with my jacket sleeve and then smoothed my short black hair down. Nothing I could do about the blood stains down the front of my jacket.

After about ten minutes, another resident of the apartments came up the walk and unlocked the front door. I tried to follow him in, but the man turned to glare at me, blocking the doorway.

"Do you live here?" he asked me, planting his feet and crossing his arms as he glared at me.

My reply caught in my dry throat. My tongue felt like sandpaper. I tried to sidle around him to the elevators, but the man threw out an arm to stop me.

"I don't think so," he said, moving closer and lifting his hand to shake his finger at my face.

I scowled and took a breath to try again to reply when the most delicious scent hit my nose—like all my favorite foods had combined into one delightful potpourri. Two sharp objects pricked my bottom lip. Without thinking, I lunged forward and bit down on the man's hand.

Liquid warmth hit my tongue. It was the most delicious thing I'd ever had in my life, yet the taste was totally indescribable. As I greedily sucked down the blood, warmth spread through me, chasing away the chill. I hadn't realized how cold I'd been until then.

My neighbor screamed and pushed me away. I stumbled backwards, but with my mouth clamped on the man's hand, I dragged him with me. We spun out onto the walk, the man beating at my head with his free hand. But between the taste and the warm feeling, he might as well have been on the moon for all I heard or felt his cries.

"Get off him!"

I was only dimly aware of the voice until someone punched my jaw, and although it didn't hurt, the shock of it made me open my mouth and let go.

"He bit me!" my neighbor slurred angrily.

I fell back a few steps before getting my feet under me. A second man, dark-skinned and wearing jeans and a leather jacket, stood in a protective stance between me and the neighbor, who was clutching his bleeding hand to his chest and beating a hasty retreat toward the apartment doors. I recognized leather jacket man as another resident of the apartments.

"What the hell were you thinking?" leather jacket growled. I narrowed my eyes at my prey getting away behind him.

There was a lump in my throat, and I was having trouble swallowing. "Thirsty," I managed to get out. The unfamiliar shape of something against my lips made it hard to talk.

I met his eyes, and then my gaze traveled lower, to his neck. To the way the vein there seemed to jump to some silent beat. I wanted it.

Growling, I darted forward. Leather jacket man crouched and spread his arms, expecting me to try to dodge around him, so he was caught unprepared by my charge. I hit him in the chest, mouth spread wide, and bit down hard on the front of his neck. He bellowed, but I barely registered the sound. More delicious nectar danced along my taste buds, commanding all of my attention.

That was until the smooth skin under my lips began to sprout hair. The shock of feeling the hair against my tongue made me let go.

I stumbled back, landing on my butt in the grass. I felt like I was well on my way to drunk. I opened my eyes to find that the man was gone. Standing in his place, on four legs and wearing the man's leather jacket and jeans, was a coyote.

"What the hell?" I sputtered in surprise as I licked my lips to get the last of the flavor off of them.

"You took the words right out of my mouth," the coyote said.

"The coyote... talked." The mugger's blow to my head must have been worse than I thought if I was hallucinating. At least the headache that had been bothering me was gone, as was that intense thirst.

The coyote put its ears back and glared at me while kicking off the jeans that were wrapped around its back legs and tail. "Are you a complete idiot? Wait, never mind. Don't answer that," the coyote said when I opened my mouth to reply.

The coyote trotted over and sat in front of me, looking incongruous in his leather jacket and shirt. "You are in so much trouble." The coyote glanced around and then back at me. I blinked stupidly at the coyote while the dew from the grass soaked into the seat of my khakis. "At least it looks like your victim made it onto the elevator before I changed. Still, I'm going to have to write you a ticket," the coyote said.

My head spun as I tried to keep up with the coyote's words. "Ticket? What?" I could see the blood staining the coyote's shirt collar, confirming that this coyote was the person I'd bitten on the neck. "What is going on?" I looked around for hidden cameras, but didn't see anything out of the ordinary in the quiet neighborhood. "Am I on a prank show?" It was the only explanation that made sense to me.

The coyote stared back at me, looking as confused as I felt with one ear cocked back and his head tilted to the side. "Who's your Maker?"

"What are you talking about?" I snapped back. Somehow this night was becoming rapidly weirder, and I didn't even understand how that was possible. "How is a coyote talking to me, anyway?"

"You." The coyote reached up with one paw and placed it over its eyes in a very human gesture. It put its paw down and sighed. "First, I'm not a coyote. I'm a jackal. Second, you can't just eat random people off the street. We have rules, young lady."

"I am not a lady, I'm a guy." My heart sunk at the misgendering, as accidental as it had been. I pushed the disappointment away and forged on. "Anyway, I didn't mean to try and eat you, or that other guy. You both just smelled," I took a deep breath, eyes fluttering closed at the memory of the smell and the taste, "delicious." All I wanted to do was go home and have a shower, followed by a stiff drink. Was that so much to ask?

"It's not for some reason. Didn't your Maker cover anything before sending you out on your first hunt?" The coyote—scratch that, the jackal looked around and then shook his head. "We shouldn't even be discussing this outside. Come on, let's go to my apartment and we'll get this sorted out." He trotted on four legs over to the jeans and tennis shoes that lay abandoned on the sidewalk, then turned to look expectantly at me. "You'll have to let me in, keys are in my front pants pocket. And bring my pants and shoes while you're at it."

I'd stash the amulet, and then get a ride to the hospital. I was obviously hurt worse than I thought if I was hallucinating talking jackals. I walked over to the jackal, picked up the jeans and shoes, and found the keys in the front pocket, just as he had said.

The jackal followed me to the front door, the corners of the jacket's unzipped sides dragging on the ground under his chest, and waited while I unlocked it. We got inside the elevator together, and before I could press the button, the jackal jumped up and bumped the five button with its nose.

When we got off the elevator, I trailed him over to an apartment door. The key from his keyring worked, and I let myself in. The jackal darted in after me. As I shut the door behind us, he said, "Just drop the pants and shoes by the door, and I'll get them later."

Shrugging, I did as the jackal said and then followed him farther into the apartment. He turned and looked up at me. "Wait on the couch, I'll be right out.

I sat on the couch, looking around. The apartment was neat and tidy, except for a dirty cup on the coffee table and a discarded magazine on the couch. I picked it up and flipped through it to see that it was all about hiking and camping. Ironic, since it was owned by a talking jackal. I snorted and tossed the magazine on the coffee table next to the dirty cup. Framed movie posters from famous action and detective films lined the walls. Given that I saw literal masterpieces every day at work, the movie posters were actually a nice change of scenery. I might have to get some for my apartment.

The man, human again, came back into the living room. He'd changed into a new dark-blue button-down shirt and dark slacks. He rubbed the side of his neck ruefully, although my teeth marks were gone.

I winced and touched my own neck. "Sorry about the..." There wasn't a delicate way to put this, so I just spit it out. "... biting. I don't know what came over me. Why aren't you bleeding anymore?"

He shot me a hard look that I couldn't read, and moved to stand in front of the coffee table with his arms crossed, looking down at me. "As a vampire, you should know better than to let yourself get so thirsty."

"I don't know what you are talking about." I threw up my hands and flopped against his cushions with a cry of frustration. "I'm not a vampire!"

"You most certainly are."

I crossed my arms and glared back at him. "Let me repeat myself. I'm. Not. A. Vampire." I ran my hands down the legs of my pants, trying to hide the way my hands started shaking at his questions and carefully avoiding touching the amulet through the cloth. "My name's Everett, by the way. Nice to meet you." I stuck out my hand.

"Jack."

Jack didn't move, just looked down at my outstretched arm, and I pulled back awkwardly. He briefly closed his eyes and reached up to massage his temple. The gesture looked better in his human form than it had when he'd done it as a jackal. He sure was handsome. I realized I was staring and glanced away, blushing.

"Okay, Everett," Jack said, moving around to sit on the chair closest to me. "I see I'll need to start at the beginning. You are a vampire. Apparently one with a very negligent Maker, but trust me. You are a vampire."

"And you're what, a werejackal?" I snorted. "That's stupid."

Jack shook his head, looking somehow both bemused and frustrated. "It's not stupid, it's the truth. Now, it's not your fault, it's your Maker who's going to get in trouble. I'm just glad I found you when I did. How many people have you drunk from?"

"I assume you mean the biting?" I asked.

Jack nodded.

"Then just you and the other guy you saw." I wondered where his questions were leading.

"Did he recognize you?"

I shook my head. "He didn't want to let me inside the building, which was how it all started, so no, I don't think he did."

"Good. Hopefully he'll just think you were a pissed off junky, rather than a vampire." Jack cocked his head, frowning. "Have you been feeling strange?"

I nodded, puzzled. "Yes, thirsty and fuzzy, with a persistent headache. It started after I was mugged earlier tonight. I'm not sure how else to describe it. I feel more alert now, though. Since I bit you two, it's like everything is in sharper focus."

"Tell me everything you remember." Jack sat forward, focused on my face.

"Why?" I froze in the act of running my hands down my pants again. The amulet hidden in my pocket felt like it weighed a thousand pounds.

Jack sighed and put his hands on his knees. "Look, I didn't want to tell you this, because I can tell you're nervous, but I'm a, well, a cop. Of sorts."

This day was just getting better and better. Now it turned out that not only was I sitting in a cop's living room with stolen loot in my pocket, also I was now a vampire? I had no idea which was worse, but at this moment I was leaning towards the former.

I licked my lips. I could still taste blood on them, and I wanted more. Jack was looking at me expectantly. "Of sorts means that you aren't a cop," I said, looking at him in what I hoped was an expression of innocence and not guilt.

"Not in the way you're used to, I expect. There's a whole supernatural society threaded through the human world. I keep the peace in that world. Punish people who don't follow the rules, help newbies, and make sure we're kept secret. Which is why I need to find out who made you and why."

I sat back, blinking. "Oh." This was even worse than I'd thought.

Jack drummed his fingers on his leg while he regarded me. Every few seconds his eyes darted up to a clock on the wall that showed that it was just past midnight.

"Do I have blood on my face?" I reached up to touch my chin.

Jack shook his head. "No, I'm sorry. I'm just trying to figure out what to do with you. I'm late for work as it is, but a newly-made vampire shouldn't be left alone."

"I don't need a babysitter," I snapped, glaring at Jack. "I'll just go home and hang out there. I need to shower and change clothes anyway."

Jack sighed and stood up. "No. I'll take you to your place so you can grab a change of clothes, but then I'm taking you to the office with me."

Crap. That would be bad. "Look, I'm not going anywhere. I'm in apartment 609 on the sixth floor. I'll hang out there. Just come by after you get off work."

"And leave you to get burned to a crisp by a stray bit of daylight coming in through your window? I don't think so. This is one of the reasons vampires get in trouble if they abandon a newbie like this. You don't realize how quick you'll go up in flames if daylight touches your skin."

Jack kept talking and I rolled my eyes, stifling a groan as I followed him into the hall. I was still having trouble believing this vampire story Jack was trying to sell me, but I couldn't figure out what he would get out of lying to me. I needed to find a way to ditch him.

CHAPTER 2

A COP, OF SORTS

ON THE ELEVATOR, JACK prattled on about proper sun-proofing procedures and I only half listened to him as I ran through possible excuses to get away from him. Only when we stepped out into the hall on the sixth floor did I remember the second part of my problem: no keys.

I eyed Jack. Nice muscle definition was visible on his arms and chest, even through the cloth of his shirt. Plus, he was a shapeshifter, and in the movies they were always super strong. He could probably just break down the door if worse came to worse. However, plan A was that knocking on the door would wake Lindsay. She might have had her phone turned off, but she was a light sleeper. She'd be pissed at being woken up, but I wouldn't have to pay out of my security deposit for a damaged door.

Jack, walking ahead of me, stopped abruptly, and I almost walked into his back. "Everett, you have a roommate?" Jack asked over his shoulder in a near whisper.

"Yeah, of course I do." I had to stop myself from rolling my eyes at Jack yet again. As if a museum intern could afford an apartment on their own. I actually could have afforded it because of my little side business, but that money was for something far more important.

"Does she usually leave the door open?"

"What? No." I pushed past Jack, unable to see past the taller man. My front door was open about a quarter of an inch. A sliver of darkness was all that was visible past the door jam.

"Get behind me," Jack hissed, and pushed me back with one hand. With his other he reached into his jacket and drew a gun.

I was so shocked that I didn't protest as Jack pushed me backwards. I hadn't realized he was armed. I wondered why a werewolf—or jackal in this case—needed a gun. Jack pressed his back against the wall of the hallway next to the door and slid along it with the gun in a two-handed grip, pointed toward the ceiling. It looked like something out of a movie. Keeping his gun in the air, Jack crouched down and leaned toward the doorway. It seemed smart to me. It put his head down at crotch level, whereas anyone who was going to shoot through the door would probably shoot higher, at chest or head height.

Jack took one hand off his gun and used it to push the door the rest of the way open. From where I was standing in the hall, I couldn't see much. Just more darkness, which itself was odd because we usually left the light in the kitchen over the sink on for midnight snack runs.

"Where's Lindsay?" I whispered, hoping she was okay. She'd been an alright roommate, and a great friend when I'd really needed one.

"Shush," Jack hissed over his shoulder. "Wait here, I'll be right back."

"Wait, shouldn't I go first? If I'm a vampire, I'm like indestructible, right? Like in the movies?"

"It's not that simple. This isn't a movie, and thinking that way will get you killed." Jack's eyes narrowed and he whipped his head back around toward my apartment, lifting his nose and scenting like a dog. Or a jackal. Wait, Jack the jackal. I snickered. What parents named a werejackal "Jack"?

"I said to be quiet. And stay here." Eyes wide, Jack disappeared into the dark of my apartment. I wondered why the sudden hurry after he'd urged such caution. Shrugging, I moved up to stand next to my door where Jack had been a moment before. I could still feel the heat from his body on the wall and smell his shampoo. A breeze whispered from my apartment, covering Jack's comforting scent with a smell that I couldn't describe, but that immediately set me on edge.

The elevator behind me dinged, and the door began to open. I glanced behind me and almost choked as I caught sight of not other tenants getting off, but two uniformed officers. When they spotted me, they both drew their guns.

Without stopping to think about it, I took two steps forward into my dark apartment, slammed the door shut behind me, and turned the deadbolt. Running on autopilot, I flipped the light switch for the front hall.

"Damn it, Everett, I told you to wait outside," Jack yelled from somewhere farther in the apartment. "Don't come any further."

"I didn't have a choice. Two cops just got off the elevator with their guns drawn and they're headed this way."

There was a pounding thump at the front door. "Police, open up."

"Shit. That other guy you bit must have called them." Jack appeared from down the hallway leading to the bedrooms. "Don't open that. We don't want them here in your condition, not to mention..." Jack trailed off as he got closer, and grabbed my arm to drag me away from the door and into the kitchen.

"But that happened outside, on the sidewalk. What are they doing up here?" I asked.

The pounding on the door was getting louder, more frantic.

"Questions later. We need to get out of here before they get in," Jack said.

"Why? I thought you were a 'cop of sorts'. Just go talk to them." I reluctantly pulled my arm from Jack's grasp.

Jack grimaced and glanced back the way he'd come from, down the hallway towards the bedrooms. "It's complicated."

Actually, it was odd that Lindsay wasn't up, especially with the banging at the door. She was a really light sleeper, up and yelling at me for the slightest noise when I got home late from fruitlessly trolling the local gay bar for dates.

"Is Lindsay home? I need to—" I moved to leave the kitchen, and Jack blocked the exit by reaching across the small space and placing a hand on either counter.

"That's part of the complication," Jack said.

"Look, just let me by." I feinted left, and then when Jack shifted, I ducked to the right under his arm. He hadn't counted on just how short I was.

Jack tried to grab my jacket, but it was like he was moving in slow motion as I ran past him. Everything felt unreal, like a dream or a slo-mo sequence from a movie. Jack's hand closed on empty air behind me as I bolted towards the bedrooms. Weird, but I didn't have time to dwell on it. The strange smell I'd detected outside got stronger as I moved farther down the hall.

I opened Lindsay's bedroom door while knocking, but stopped cold at the sight that greeted me there.

Lindsay lay on her back on her bed, her eyes open and glazed. The bed was red with pooling blood that had run down from the wide slash that ran all the way across her neck.

I tried to scream, but Jack ran up behind me and clamped a hand over my mouth, muffling my cry.

"Shh," Jack whispered into my ear. "It's okay, but you can see why we can't be here when those cops come in. We need to get out of here, now."

"Shit, shit," I said, pushing away Jack's hand. Now that Jack had distracted me from the body, I noticed that Lindsay's room had been trashed. All the clothes from her closet were scattered on the floor, and the dresser drawers were all askew and empty, the contents thrown about the room. When I thought about it, when I'd run through the living room, it had been a mess too. Oh, no. My stash. I had to check on it.

"We can go out the window," Jack said.

I let Jack pull me away and shut the door to Lindsay's room. The pounding on the door had gone silent, which was somehow more ominous than the banging.

"I need to check my room," I hissed to Jack, darting past him to my door at the end of the hall. Jack chased after me, but again I was faster.

As I grabbed the doorknob, I heard the front door crashing open. "Police! Freeze!"

I couldn't see the front door from the hall, but they'd seen me come inside so they knew someone was here.

"Go, go!" Jack hissed, pushing me into my bedroom ahead of him and carefully easing the door shut behind us. Jack turned and leaned against the door, pressing his ear against it.

I reached over to flip on the light, but Jack glanced at me and shook his head. I pulled my hand back. I could see well enough anyway. Dim light from the streetlights below came in through the windows where I had failed to fully close the blinds when I'd left for work. Was it only this morning? It seemed like it had been ages since I'd last been home. So much had happened since then.

My room was as trashed as Lindsay's had been. My dresser drawers had been pulled out, and my closet had been emptied all over the floor and bed. Even my posters had been ripped off the wall. My eyes darted to the AC vent on the floor by my bed where I kept my stash of artifacts stolen from the museum. The vent cover was missing, and the plastic bags that I'd been using to store the items were tossed on the floor, empty. They'd been taped inside the vent, out of sight of anyone casually peering inside. Someone had either known where to look, or done a very thorough search.

I was in trouble. I owed those items to the boss, and she wasn't going to be happy I had lost them. I physically grabbed my right arm with my left hand to stop myself from feeling for the amulet in my pocket to check that it was still there. If I was right, what I had there might make up for the missing items. If I was wrong, well, I was in a lot more trouble than I thought.

"What happened in here?" I whispered.

"I don't know, but we need to leave before the men out there find us in here," Jack hissed to me. "We can talk about the how and why later."

"Fine," I whispered back. I started stepping over the wreckage of my room. I spotted my testosterone prescription bottle in the mess and scooped it up without stopping, stuffing the little vial in my jacket pocket and zipping it closed.

Jack unlatched the window and pushed it open, letting in the cool night air. He grabbed the sides of the screen and twisted it out, letting it go to drop out into the night. It was a very long drop to the grass below. Jack grabbed my arm and shoved me at the window. I grabbed the window sill and tried not to look down, feeling a little faint. It had started raining since we'd come inside, and rain droplets pattered my face and hands.

"Jump," Jack urged in a whisper, glancing nervously over his shoulder at the closed bedroom door.

"What? Are you crazy? I'll break a leg or worse," I whispered back.

"You're a vampire. You'll be fine. Now hurry!"

He seemed so sure of himself. Sighing, I put my hands on the ledge, preparing to climb out, but caught sight of the ground below and froze.

"Hurry!" Jack urged. "We don't have time."

"I can't, it's too high!" I squeezed my eyes shut and tried to back away, but Jack shoved me forward.

The door behind us banged open. "Freeze, police! Put your hands where we can see them and step away from the window." Their voices were muffled. I think they were in Lindsay's room across the hall. It'd only be moments before they found us.

I startled and would have backed away, except for Jack standing right behind me. My pulse raced.

"Shit. Sorry."

I wanted to ask what he was sorry for when Jack's hands moved down to my hips, grabbing my pants and lifting me up. "Out you go!" Jack hefted, flinging me up and out.

"No!" I shrieked, flailing for the window frame as the ground came into view. My fingernails scratched the paint on the window frame on my way out, but I didn't manage to get a grip with Jack's continued pushing at my butt and legs.

Next thing I knew I was falling, spinning through the air as wind rushed past me. I felt almost weightless as I spun in freefall, at least until I landed on my back on the grass behind the apartment building. The impact knocked the breath out of me and I felt my spine snap. It hurt, but not as much as I would have expected. I felt another pop and gritted my teeth against the wave of pain that wracked me.

I opened my eyes in time to see Jack jump straight out of the window like a superhero, sailing easily over my position. Without thinking I rolled over to watch him, enthralled by the sight. The vial in my pocket shattered as I rolled over it, and the oily residue soaked through the windbreaker. Shit.

Jack landed in a crouch that turned into a roll about ten feet away from the building. It looked as if he'd just jumped from a burning or exploding building in a movie scene, a comparison not at all harmed by his rugged good looks and muscled physique. He sprang to his feet as if he'd just done a somersault, not jumped from the sixth floor. "Follow me, I'm parked up this way." He jerked his head to indicate the far end of the building. Without watching to see if I followed him, he jogged off toward the sidewalk.

"I can't, I think I broke my back," I called after him.

Jack slowed and turned, but didn't stop, continuing to walk backwards. "You're fine. You're a vampire. You're already healed."

I sat up, and Jack was right. The pain was gone and nothing felt broken. Maybe... maybe Jack was telling the truth and I was a vampire now.

My head spun. I thought through my options and realized I had none. My work had been compromised, and so had my apartment. Jack was an unknown element. As long as Lindsay's killer remained unaware of Jack, I might have a chance of staying safe. I also needed to keep Jack from finding out about the stolen amulet. Cursing, I climbed to my feet to run after him, wiping grass from the back of my damp jeans.

CHAPTER 3

SOCIAL WORK FOR WEREWOLVES

WHEN WE GOT TO the sidewalk, Jack slowed down to a walk, allowing me to catch up to him. After I joined Jack, he didn't quicken his pace.

He must have caught my questioning expression, because he said, "Less suspicious." He pulled out a cellphone and called a contact as we walked to the corner. "Jack here." Pause. "Yeah, sorry." He glanced at me. "I got caught up with an incident at my apartment building. I'll be there soon. Oh, and I'm bringing a guest with me."

Another pause as Jack listened to someone on the other end. I tried to overhear, but either vampire hearing wasn't as great as the movies made it out to be, or Jack had the volume turned down really low.

"No, I can't help it. Look, I have a favor to ask while I drive over there. Some cops were at my building, at the apartment of Everett..." He trailed off and looked at me, one eyebrow raised.

"Boesch. Everett Boesch," I said, finally catching on to what Jack needed. I spelled it out, which Jack dutifully repeated into the phone.

Jack listened to the person on the other end for a moment. We turned the corner and Jack pulled out keys with his free hand, and pushed a button on the key fob. The lights on a Toyota Camry four-door sedan blinked. Jack stepped off the sidewalk and walked around to the driver's side door.

I opened the passenger door, sliding inside in time to hear, "Yes, that does have to do with why I'm late. Look, find out anything you can. Thanks." Jack pulled the phone away from his ear and ended the call.

"You didn't tell them about my, uh...vampire thing." I looked at him expectantly as he slid his key into the ignition.

Jack grimaced and pulled away from the curb. "Yeah. That was on purpose. If I did, he'd tell the head of the city and they'd whisk you away. But we need to find out who is after you first. It wouldn't do for me to save your life and then accidentally end up turning you over to the very people who might be after you."

"You don't trust the vampires?" I cocked my head and looked at Jack, keeping half an eye on the road, trying to work out where he was taking me.

Jack snorted. "I'm a lycanthrope; we never trust vampires."

"Okay, now that you're on the way to work, will you please tell me more about what is going on?" I twisted in my seat to look at Jack, realizing I didn't need to watch the road. Where we were going didn't really matter. I was a fugitive from the law, probably didn't have a job anymore, and had no family to turn to—they'd almost all turned their backs on me when I'd announced my transition. Then there was the whole vampire thing that I still needed Jack to explain to me.

Jack grimaced. "It's complicated."

"Like a cop," I said, making air quotes with both hands. "So how is it complicated? Get talking."

"We don't work directly with the human police, although we do have contacts and plants on the force. I used to be a cop..." He sighed. "But I'm not anymore."

I stayed silent, waiting for the rest, but apparently Jack had said all he wanted to say. Jack's expression and hunched shoulders told me I shouldn't press him about what changed.

"Are you alright?" Jack asked me quietly in an abrupt change of subject, glancing at me as he drove through the quiet streets of southeast Portland's neighborhood towards the freeway.

"Besides scared out of my mind?" I let out a strained laugh. "I'm doing great." I felt panic bubble up, but pushed it down and plastered on a smile.

"I mean after seeing your roommate like that... Were you two close?"

"Yes, but I don't want to think about that now. Can we talk about something else? I need a distraction. Like, what now?" I asked. I realized I had started to babble, and my hands were shaking. I snapped my mouth closed and took a few deep breaths to try to calm myself. Now that Jack had brought it up again, I couldn't help but remember the way Lindsay's eyes had blankly stared up at me.

"Now? You're my newest client." Jack sighed again, deeper this time, and paused to take a left-hand turn. "I help acclimate new shapeshifters to the change, introduce them to the new rules they'll have to follow, that sort of thing."

I stared at him. "Seriously? You're a supernatural shapeshifter with jaw dropping good looks, and you're a social-worker?"

Jack let out a startled laugh. "Jaw dropping, huh?"

"You heard me," I stammered. Crap, I couldn't believe I'd said that out loud. I reddened, but set my expression to be as neutral as I could manage and nodded. The way Jack's eyes sparkled as he flashed a quick smile my way made my stomach flutter.

"What would you have me do? Run around Portland in tights rescuing damsels in distress?" We'd stopped at a light so Jack turned his head to smirk at me.

"You rescued me," I said without thinking. Jack's smirk deepened, and I realized what I'd just implied. "I mean," I backpedaled furiously, "you should use your powers for good, to help people—"

"I am helping people, the best way I can." Jack's voice hardened and raised as he spoke. "I was a cop for five years before, well, before I had to retire. Trust me. Keeping the newbies off the cop's radar and out of the public's attention is a very important job." Something about what I had said struck a nerve. Another topic I made a mental note to avoid.

"Okay, okay. I'm sorry. Let's get back to the topic at hand. You said you help shapeshifters, but according to you, I'm a vampire. So how can I pretend to be your newest client?"

Jack shrugged. "We'll just say you're a shapeshifter. No one will notice."

"But won't your office-mates smell that I'm a fraud?"

"Let me ask you something. Since you turned, how much has your sense of smell increased?"

"What?" I stared at Jack, but decided to humor him. I took a tentative sniff of the air. The car smelled like Jack and the pine air freshener that hung from the rear-view mirror, nothing more. "Seems the same. But you're a werewolf. Jackal, I mean," I amended hastily when Jack shot me a side-glare without taking his eyes off the road.

"My jackal form may have better senses, but my human senses didn't change. I'm just a little stronger and faster than I was. Same with you. You're just slightly deader than you were. Maybe a little paler. Just don't try to eat anyone and no one will catch on."

"But you sniffed in the hallway, I saw it."

"Human noses are more sensitive than you might realize."

"That's disappointing." I slumped in my seat and turned my head to watch the raindrops rolling down the window. "I died and became a vampire, and all I got was really thirsty." Okay, thirstier. I licked my dry lips. The few gulps I'd gotten from Jack and the other man earlier had helped at the time, but all this running around had brought the parched feeling back.

Jack chuckled. "What'dya want, a T-shirt?"

"Seeing as how I'm currently not wearing a shirt under this jacket, that'd be a nice start." It had been soaked with blood, so I'd tossed it before walking home.

Jack made a coughing sound, and I thought I saw Jack's cheeks darkened. Or felt it, more like. I almost swore I could see the glow of his blood in his veins. "I can find you something at the office. We keep spares for the shifters. Seriously though, Everett." Jack glanced at me again. "How thirsty are you?"

"Not as bad as it was when I bit you," I said, licking my lips again, "but enough to be noticeable. Why? Are you worried?"

Jack frowned. "A little. You were thirsty enough to attack that other man and me, but you didn't get much from either of us. I don't know much about new vampires, and that worries me. I do know that the vampire clans keep the new ones sequestered at first, and during that time they are only allowed out while supervised by an elder, which makes me think they're dangerous. But you seem rational, mostly. If the feeling gets worse, tell me."

I nodded, and then, realizing that Jack might not have seen the gesture because he was driving, said, "I will."

We drove in silence for a bit. I sat back, thinking about what Jack had just said, squashing my disappointment that Jack couldn't tell me more about my new state. After the events in my apartment, I was now more inclined to believe him.

The silence was broken by Jack's phone ringing as we exited the freeway just north of downtown. The sound came through the car's speakers and was loud enough that I jumped.

Jack held a finger to his lips. I nodded and made a zipping motion across my lips as Jack pressed a button on the steering wheel.

"Hello, Stacy. Sorry I'm running so late, but I'm almost at the office."

"Well, turn right around." The woman's voice came through the car's speakers, loud and clear. "Dave just intercepted a call about a confused fox approaching people out east near that outlet mall in Wood Village." She rattled off an address.

"Got it," Jack said. We were in the industrial area of town north of downtown, and at this time of night the streets were all but deserted. Jack flipped a quick U-turn and we sped back the way we'd come. "I'll call and give you an update when I get there," he said, and then punched a button on the dash to end the call.

"What was that about?" I asked. "Why send you off to chase after a fox? Shouldn't animal control take care of something like that?"

"If we determine it's just a regular fox, sure, we'll leave it to them. But it could be a newly-changed shapeshifter, and if it is, I need to get them somewhere safe and get them help." Jack pressed the accelerator and the car shot forward—much different than the leisurely pace he'd driven at before.

"And if it is, but animal control gets there first?" I asked.

"Let's hope you don't have to find out."

CHAPTER 4

THE WEREFOX

THE ADDRESS JACK'S BOSS sent us to turned out to be a Target store. Jack parked at the back of the nearly-empty lot in front of the closed store.

"So, what can I do to help?" I asked, getting out as I scanned the little patch of trees at the edge of the lot. The rain had stopped and the clouds were starting to clear.

"You can wait in the car," Jack said as he went around to the trunk and popped it open, hiding him from view.

"I want to help. I can help." I walked to the rear of the car and stopped abruptly. Jack was shirtless, the curves of his muscles under his brown skin accented by the pale moonlight.

He unbuttoned his pants, then smirked at me as he unzipped them. "Could you give me a little privacy?"

I blushed, but didn't move. "What's with the floor show?"

Jack paused with his thumbs hooked over the waistband of his jeans. "It's the fastest way to confirm if this fox is really a fox or shapeshifted human. Remember what we were talking about in the car, about scent?"

"I get it. In your jackal form, you can sniff out the fox faster than us beating around in the bushes."

"I'll also be able to tell as soon as I find the fox if it's a shapeshifter or not." At that he pulled his pants and underwear down in one motion. He stepped out of his jeans, already barefoot. Jack finished stripping off his pants and then lifted them up, sadly hiding his assets from view, to dig around in the front pocket. He pulled out his keys and tossed them to me.

It looked like the keys were moving in slow motion as they tumbled through the air; I had all the time in the world to lift my hand up and catch them. As soon as my fingers closed around the keys, time seemed to snap back to its usual speed.

Jack lifted one eyebrow at me. "Ha, between this and the way you outran me in the apartment, it looks like you're getting the hang of 'vampire speed'." He tossed his jeans and underwear in the trunk over his shirt and shoes, and then slammed the lid closed.

"... thanks." I could not tear my eyes from Jack's naked form. I was sure my face was bright red now, even if I didn't feel flushed. Jack was gorgeous, it was true, and it didn't help that I hadn't been on a date in years, but it felt a little rude to be staring like this. Still, I couldn't pull my eyes away.

"I shouldn't be too long. You're welcome to turn the car on listen to music while you wait, but don't answer the phone if it rings."

I opened my mouth to protest, but before I could, Jack's form started to shift, getting blurry on the edges as he sprouted fur and shrunk. A moment later, a jackal stood on all fours in Jack's place. The jackal gave me one long look, as if to say "get back in the car already", and then trotted off into the underbrush at the edge of the parking lot.

Feeling useless, I stuffed Jack's keys in my pocket and got back in the passenger seat. During the ride over I'd been focused on talking with Jack. Now that I was just sitting here, idly tapping my fingers on my knees, my thirst seemed to grow worse by the second. I wished I had my phone, or a book, or one of my art magazines to distract myself.

Bored, I looked around Jack's car. Scratches and tears covered the fabric of the back seats, yet the rest of the car was neat and clean. Traffic went by in the distance, more than I would've expected given the late hour. Everything seemed so normal, so calm. My whole world had been turned upside down and inside out... yet the world continued on as it had been.

A scratch at the door of the car brought me out of my reverie. I sat up and opened the door. Jack's jackal form stood there, giving me the side-eye with one ear cocked back, and holding a struggling fox in his muzzle by the scruff of its neck. When the fox caught sight of me, it began shrieking. The high pitched scream that came from the fox sounded more like a human child in pain than an animal.

I winced and covered my ears. For some reason I always thought foxes barked, like dogs, not this horrible screaming. "I take it the fox is a shapeshifter?" I yelled over the noise.

Jack nodded and then jerked his head towards the back door. The jackal backed up enough to let me get out of the car. I opened the back door and the jackal hopped in, still holding the much-smaller fox in his mouth. I shut the door behind them and was moving to get into the passenger seat, when I paused and looked back at Jack. He couldn't drive like that, not while restraining the fox in the back seat. I poked my head through the open passenger door, leaned into the car, and looked at the pair. Jack was trying to hold down the squirming fox, but was having a hard time of it.

"Do you need me to drive?" I yelled over the fox's screams, pulling Jack's keys out of my pocket and holding them up. "I don't have a license, though. I mean, I know how, but my license was in my wallet, which was stolen."

Jack growled and shook his head. He managed to get the fox underneath of him, pinned under his much bigger bulk so he could let go of the fox's scruff. "No. There's a CD case under your seat. Get out Music for Meditation, turn the car on, and put it in the player." Like earlier that night, it was very disconcerting to hear a human's voice coming from a jackal's muzzle.

"Why isn't it talking, like you?" I yelled back, covering my ears.

"Takes practice to talk in animal form. Now, CD, please? She can't turn back until she calms down."

The case was right were he said it would be. I put in the CD and moments later, soothing piano music filled the car, although it could hardly be heard over the fox's continued screams. In the back, the fox clawed and snapped at Jack, but the angle was wrong and mostly it tore more holes in the seat. Jack leaned over it, mouth next to its ear, whispering something too low for me to catch.

"So I guess it's a myth that weres only change on the full moon?" I asked as I watched them. The music didn't seem to be helping the fox calm down at all. At least it finally stopped screaming.

Jack didn't answer, so I sighed and sat back to look up through the windshield at the sky overhead. A few dark clouds obscured some of the stars—the last of what remained of the rainclouds from earlier—but they were quickly being blown away. We were far enough outside Portland that I could see a few twinkling dots over the light pollution. Half a crescent moon hung high in the sky, shining brightly. That was answer enough to my question, I supposed. Movies had gotten that wrong about werewolves—or in this case, werejackals and werefoxes—and that made me wonder what they'd gotten wrong about vampires. I guess that was why Jack had warned me to stop thinking in those terms.

The CD played through twice before the fox calmed down. A few times I tried to ask questions, but Jack didn't answer any of them, focused on whispering to the fox, so I eventually fell silent, nervously looking at the sky in the east, watching for the telltale glow of coming sunrise. Without my phone, I couldn't research what time sunrise would happen at.

Jack must have seen the direction of my glances, because he said, "Don't worry, we have time."

A few cars drove past us in the parking lot, coming from behind the Target. They glanced curiously at the car and me, but no one stopped to bother us.

I licked my dry lips, trying to ignore my growing thirst. I began humming along with the piano music, making up lyrics in my head to distract myself.

Finally the fox shuddered, its form twisting. Jack sat up, moving off the fox to crouch next to it as it changed back. Its fur pulled back in and its limbs grew until a naked, young, blonde woman sat crouched on all fours in the seat. She flushed and curled back into a fetal position, pulling her legs to her chest to huddle up against the back driver's-side door, as far from Jack and me as she could get. Her eyes welled and tears began falling silently down her cheeks before she buried her face in her knees.

A warmth hit my face from her direction, and I wanted to close my eyes and bask in it. I couldn't keep my eyes off her. It was like feeling the bright sun for the first time after a gray Portland winter. I sat up and knelt in the seat, leaning into the back. She seemed to pulse with life, and everything else in the car fell away. I traced the red lines under her skin with my eyes.

Someone was talking. I registered the sound, but it had no meaning. Something cracked across my face, snapping my head to the side. My eye contact with the girl was broken as my face was mashed against the driver's side headrest. I was halfway into the back seat, kneeling on the center console, but I didn't remember moving.

"Everett, stop!" Jack yelled in my ear.

I screwed my eyes shut and took a deep breath to calm myself. That was a mistake. Jack's musky sweat filled my nose—almost, but not quite, overwhelming my sense of self again. I could feel something in my mouth growing and pressing down on my lips. Two tiny pin-pricks of sensation. I took another shuddering breath, breathing through my mouth this time, before trying to speak.

"I'm okay now. Please, let me go." I slurred a little around the new fangs. I ran my tongue along them, wondering why I hadn't noticed them earlier. Although I had been a little—no, a lot out of it at the time. I barely even remembered biting Jack, only the warmth and taste of the blood. Thinking of that was a mistake; my thirst increased, my mouth so dry I felt dizzy.

"Are you sure?" Jack's voice was hard, but I detected a hint of worry underneath the gruff tone.

I nodded, or tried to, but Jack's hand on my face stopped me. "Yes. I'm good now. I've got it under control."

"Alright, then."

Jack's hand withdrew, and eyes still closed tight, I backed away and turned around to slide back down into the passenger seat. The back of my head and the left side of my face felt warmth still coming from Jack and the woman.

The back seat creaked, and the car rocked as Jack moved back. "Do up your seatbelt too, Everett."

Jack didn't trust me to not lose control again, and I didn't blame him. I didn't trust myself at the moment. I sighed, but did as I was told. Jack's warmth shifted, accompanied by the sounds of movement from the backseat and the thump of something opening.

"Here, you can put these on," Jack said to the girl. "And I've got tissues, too."

I practiced my breathing, doing meditation exercises that I'd learned in PE class in high school. The pressure on my lips lessoned as I calmed down, and my fangs retracted.

"Thanks. My name is Emily," the woman said, her voice quaking. There was a pause, and the sounds of a person getting dressed in a tight space. "What's his problem? And what was wrong with his eyes? "

Eyes? Nothing was wrong with my eyes, was there? I sat up, opening my eyes, and flipped down the visor above my seat to look in the mirror there. My eyes, so dark-brown people mistook them for black, looked back at myself, framed by a few wisps of my short, messy, black hair. That I could see myself shot down another myth that vampires didn't have a reflection.

"And I don't smell it now, but before, when I was smaller, he smelled wrong. It scared me."

Shrugging, I closed the visor, catching a quick glimpse of Jack and the girl on the seat behind me as it closed. Jack had on jeans and was just pulling on a T-shirt, and the girl now wore a very baggy black sweatshirt and pants. A box of tissues sat in her lap. Her eyes were puffy and she was dabbing at her face with a soggy tissue. The center of the back seat was down, revealing a hole through to the trunk, which explained where they'd gotten the clothes from.

I was tempted to look back and glare at her, but just that one glimpse of her in the back seat in the mirror had caused my jaw to tighten and ache.

Jack said something under his breath in a language I didn't know, but from the tone I guessed it was a swear.

"This night," he muttered under his breath. Then louder, he said, "Yeah, sorry about that. It'll be easier to calm down to change back next time, when he isn't around. Normally it isn't quite that difficult. But he's here because, like you, he's a supernatural who also just discovered what he is tonight."

"At least I can't smell it anymore." Disgust dripped from her words.

I was tempted to respond with a jab about foxes and their ear-piercing screams, but my fangs were back, pressing down on my lower lip.

"Speaking of which, Everett, you good?" Jack asked.

I closed my eyes again, clamping my jaw shut. "No," I whispered.

"Shit," Jack hissed. The car creaked as he moved, and something cool and round tapped my shoulder. "Here, drink this. It will help tide you over until I can get you something at the office." I took the bottle, recognizing the distinctive shape of a Gatorade bottle.

"Gatorade, really?" I laughed, even as I unscrewed the cap by feel and began chugging it. The cool liquid felt good on my parched tongue, but the taste made me gag. Like drinking rotten fruit. Still, I downed the whole thing. Jack and Emily were talking in the back, but I was so focused on the sweet, cool bite of the beverage easing my thirst that I barely heard them.

A door slammed, and a moment later the driver's door opened and the car bounced as Jack got in. "Here," he said when I lowered the empty bottle. "Lay this over your face while I drive. It will help." The empty bottle was pulled from my hand and replaced with a dry cloth.

"Where are we going?" Emily asked from the back seat, her voice shaky.

Jack replied while I leaned my seat back. "My office. I work for PCA, the Paranormal Creature Alliance. We help people like you and Everett here who are new to the supernatural world."

"Oh." Emily fell silent and Jack started the car.

I kept my eyes closed and leaned back against the headrest, placing the fabric—I suspected from the smell and feel that it was one of Jack's T-shirts—over my face. Immediately I was enveloped by Jack's musky smell. Smiling, I put both my hands on it and pressed it into my nose, inhaling deeply.

I relaxed back, letting the warm piano music, the roar of the tires on the road, and the scent of Jack lull me into a doze.

CHAPTER 5

THE PARANORMAL CREATURE ALLIANCE

THE SLOWING OF THE car as it got off the freeway bumped me awake. I hadn't meant to fall asleep. I sat up and rubbed my eyes, inadvertently dropping the T-shirt from my face onto my lap. We were on Highway 30, heading north. The trees of Forest Park on the left were nothing but dark blots, broken occasionally by the glow of street lamps.

I glanced in the back seat. Emily sat with her knees pulled up to her chin and her arms wrapped around them, staring silently out the driver's side window. That damned meditation piano music was still playing. The clock said 4:45 AM. I glanced at the sky, but it was still pitch black outside.

The St. John's Bridge became visible in the distance, the lights on it combined with the dark void that was the river far below made it look like it was a bridge through space, leading to the stars. However, instead of continuing on, Jack took a left at the light before the bridge turnout, into the parking lot of a car tow business just south of the bridge. It was a long, narrow lot that ran north to south, bordered by Forest Park on the west and Highway 30 on the east.

I'd seen it from the bus before, but hadn't really noticed it before except to wonder why it had its own stoplight.

"I think they're closed," I said after Jack stopped at the closed chainlink fence that blocked off the parking lot from the traffic on the highway. There was just enough space between the fence and the road for his car to not be hit by the sparse southbound early morning traffic on the highway.

Jack shot me a half-smile and reached up to press the button on a garage door opener attached to the visor. "Are they?" The gate began rattling slowly open, rolling to the side parallel to the rest of the fence. Jack drove in once there was enough space for the car. After we were inside, he pressed the button again and the gate closed behind us.

He drove past a dark building that had the logo of a tow company on the glass door, and turned down a gravel path that ran between the two lines of wrecked cars that ran the length of the lot, bordered by the highway on one side and the trees of Forest Park on the other. A chainlink fence topped with barbed wire encircled the lot.

Jack said, "The tow business is a cover for our offices. Handily explains all the traffic in and out, and provides some income to keep us going. Not like we can exactly get government funding for supernatural social services, and the fines from tickets only cover so much."

"I hadn't considered that," I said.

When we reached the middle of the line of cars, Jack made a hard right turn, squeezing through a space between two of the cars. Jack slowed down, but kept driving.

"Stop!" I yelled, pointing at the fence.

In the back, Emily shrieked, and I was tempted to join her, but instead reached out and grabbed the door, bracing myself for impact as the car's bumper reached the trees. The cheap plastic cracked under my grip.

However, rather than crashing, the car kept going. The image of the fence and trees in front of us wavered like a heat mirage before vanishing. The crunch of gravel under the tires was replaced with the smooth feel of asphalt. I blinked, and Emily's scream trailed off.

Jack laughed uproariously at our reaction. If I could have pried my hands from the door handle, I would have been tempted to punch his arm. "Best part of bringing newbies here." Jack chuckled.

I twisted around to look behind us. The illusion of the trees was back in place, making it look like the road appeared from nowhere. Even the light filtering through from the tow lot's floodlamps showed shadows from the illusionary trees. Despite the fact that I was now a vampire and had met both a real life werefox and werejackal, I hadn't ever considered that might mean magic was real too.

It was pitch black. Trees lined both sides of the single-lane road which, combined with the car's headlamps, turned the road into a tunnel through the dark. We drove for another few minutes up the hill. The road took a sharp turn around a switchback and then a red brick building came into view, lights blazing from the windows around the closed blinds.

Jack pulled up and parked along a line of cars at the side of the building, then turned off the car. "Last stop, everyone out."

"Where's this?" Emily asked sharply from the back seat.

"A safe space, like I said." Jack got out of the car. "Come with me. Both of you."

I got out, walked around the car, and stood near the trunk. Jack got out and opened the driver's-side rear door to help Emily out. She shook, leaning heavily on his arm.

"The first transformation is always the hardest," Jack said, shutting her door behind her. He nodded his head to me and said, "After you."

I shrugged and walked around the building to the front door. Jack and Emily stumbled along more slowly behind me. The unmarked doors were made of thick steel. I tugged on them, but they didn't budge.

A speaker next to the door buzzed and a crackly voice asked, "Who the fuck are you?"

"Jack brought me," I said, glancing around until I spotted a camera above the speaker.

"He's with me," Jack said as he and Emily came up the steps behind me.

The door pinged and the lock clicked open. I pulled the handle and held it open, waiting while Jack half-carried Emily through, then followed them inside.

A young man looked up from the receptionist desk. A screen to the side of him showed a view of the front porch. "Jack, took you long enough. You call in late, then one fox call that should have been an hour job at most takes you all night, and then you come back with two people? Boss is pissed. She wants to see you, now. Hope you have a good explanation for it all."

Jack sighed and nodded to the man. "All right, let me just get these two settled first, Dave."

Dave shrugged and spun to the side, bending over and going back to watch his monitors.

"This way." Jack pushed through a swinging door on the wall to the left of the reception desk, carrying Emily with him. I followed him.

This room was set up like a living room, with a couch against the far wall that was flanked by two plush reclining chairs, and a small coffee table in front of them. The wall opposite the setup had a counter with dorm-sized fridge and a coffee station. Another door exited the other side.

Jack set Emily down on the couch, and I sat on one of the chairs. Jack went over to the fridge and pulled out two Gatorade bottles. "Drink those."

He tossed one each to Emily and me. Like earlier, time seemed to slow as the bottle flew towards me. I caught it easily, twisted the cap off, and took a big swig. This one was also like drinking rotten fruit. I gagged and almost spit it out.

"Nasty. This is the same, awful flavor you gave me in the car." I made a face and looked at the label. "What the? This is my favorite flavor, or at least it was." I made a face and put the cap back on.

"I know it tastes bad now in your new state, but drink it. The nutrients will help hold off your thirst."

Jack turned to leave back the way we'd come, but then glanced at the clock on the wall above the couch and cursed. "No, wait, we don't have time. Emily, you wait here. Everett, you come with me."

Sighing, I stood up. Emily still looked scared, her eyes still red-rimmed yet dry, but she nodded. Jack turned around and went over to the other door out of the room, pulled out a key, and unlocked it.

"This way."

"Why's it locked?" The room on the other side was tiny, more of a hallway than a room. Two doors were on the far wall opposite the one we'd come through, and a third door was to the right.

"More to protect the people in the waiting room from wandering in here than anything. In here." Jack unlocked the leftmost door and opened it, gesturing inside.

The room, more like a closet, had two camping bunks with trunks pushed underneath, a rickety old wooden nightstand between them, and nothing else. Not even any windows.

I sighed and glumly contemplated the cots. "Really? Camping bunks? I thought vampires slept in coffins."

"Nothing is stopping you if you want to get one, but other vampires will make fun of you." Jack put a comforting hand on my shoulder. My heart jumped into my throat at his touch, warm and comforting. "I know it's not much. If I'd had more time I could have gotten you put up in one of our safe houses, but it'll have to do for tonight."

"It's—it's fine," I stuttered over my words as his hand slid off my shoulder. I sidled further into the room and turned to face Jack. The events of the night were starting to catch up to me and hugged myself tightly, closing my eyes to stop the tears that I could feel threatening me.

Jack stepped closer, bending over and wrapping his arms around me in a loose hug. "We'll get to the bottom of this, I promise."

"Thank you. But what now?" I stifled a sob and hugged him back, overwhelmed by the events of the night. He was warm, and I could hear his heartbeat pounding loudly near my face. My senses seemed sharper, my hearing better—or I was imagining also being able to feel each beat of his pulse against my face and arms.

"You are going to stay in here and get some rest. I'm going to go talk to my boss." Jack's arms squeezed me briefly, and then he let go. He put a hand on my cheek, giving me a sad smile that I couldn't read before stepping back. I missed his comforting warmth already, and had to stop myself from trailing after him.

"And in the morning?" I asked, grabbing my arms with my hands to keep from reaching for him again.

A corner of Jack's mouth twitched. I realized what I'd said and blushed.

"Vampires don't really do mornings. I'll be back for you this evening, and we'll talk about next steps then." Jack started to close the door. "Oh, there are sheets and pillows in the trunks under the beds. Don't leave this room until I come to get you. The sun comes up soon, and this room is light-proofed."

Jack closed the door, and the lock clicked.

I made the bed, got undressed, and lay down. I twisted and turned on the uncomfortable camp cot, trying to get to sleep. I was so thirsty it hurt. Choking down the rest of that Gatorade hadn't helped much, or at least not as much as the first one had.

For a while I lay there, eyes closed, concentrating on feeling the sunrise, but I didn't feel anything except my dry throat and rumbling stomach.

With the lights shut off and no windows, it was pitch black in here— not even stray light from under the door—but then Jack had said this room had been light-proofed. Sighing and unable to sleep, I pulled the amulet out of my pocket and began idly turning it around in my hands. I drifted off as I rubbed the face of the amulet.

CHAPTER 6

BLOOD MEMORIES

I RODE IN THE passenger seat of a car as a rainy evening flashed by the windows. I didn't recognize the driver or the streets. It wasn't Portland, that much I was sure of, since the look of the trees were unfamiliar to me. The woman in the driver's seat wore a blue suit that emphasized the red of her hair, which was pulled back into a loose ponytail at the base of her neck. She flashed me a smile and opened her mouth to talk, when the crackly squawk of a radio cut her off.

"10-13, 10-13. Active shooter at the Petunia Apartments. Subject is a white male. Armed with a handgun. Multiple shots fired."

I reached out to pick up the handset, only my skin was a warm brown color, much different than my cooler pale skin, and hairier. The kind of hair that I hoped to grow on T. I wanted to stop and examine it, but the dream pulled me along. This was nothing like my usual dreams. Everything felt so grounded and real, more like a vivid memory than anything else.

"Officers Prashad and Kelly responding," I heard myself say into the handset.

Prashad? Who was that? While I struggled to make sense of what was going on, Officer Kelly—now that I looked closer I confirmed that the blue suit was, in fact, a police officer's uniform complete with name badge—turned on the car and sirens. It wasn't a long drive. They talked some, but I was too disoriented to catch much beyond that Officer Kelly's first name was Andre.

We pulled up to a cluster of police cars with flashing lights parked in front a two-story apartment building—the kind with open-air walkways that looked out over the parking lot. I parked near the rest and got out of the car, drawing my gun. A growing knot of dread was forming in my gut. I strained to stop myself from getting out of the car, but I had no control of my body in the dream.

I caught sight of my face in the side view mirror as I got out, and was shocked to recognize it as Jack's. Straining to stop myself, I drew my gun, crouch-walking across the pavement with the gun pointed at the ground to join Andre, along with a six other cops crouched behind the stairwell.

A Sargent was in the middle of a debrief of the situation. He nodded curtly to Kelly and me as we arrived, but didn't interrupt his speech.

"The suspect has barricaded himself in one of the second-floor apartments with two hostages: his kid and ex-wife. We don't know if they are still alive. You two," he bobbed his head toward us, "head around the back and keep watch, make sure he doesn't find another way out."

"Yes, sir," I said. We took off at a jog, guns held low, heading around the corner. The side of the building was in shadow, but enough light came from the corner streetlight that we didn't need our flashlights. Neat squares of light shone into the alley behind the building from the apartments.

Andre rounded the corner first. There was the short crack of a gunshot and he fell back into view, his face covered in blood that poured from a jagged hole in his forehead. I screamed and lunged to catch him before he hit the ground. Andre's brown eyes were wide in death and stared up past my face vacantly.

Footsteps thudded on pavement, and I looked up to see a man with a gun running away from us down the alley behind the apartments. I let Andre's body fall and brought up my gun, blinking back tears. The man glanced over his shoulder. He pointed his gun back and fired off several rounds in a series of sharp cracks. One hit my body armor in the center, and the impact was enough to knock the breath out of me. The second shot went wide, pinging off the bricks next to my head. Shrapnel hit my cheeks and nose, drawing blood. I shot, but missed. My shot hit the bricks a few inches behind the running figure.

The man got off one more shot, and this one hit me in the lower neck, just missing the edge of the body armor. My world filled with pain. I tried to scream, but all that came out was a burble of blood. The taste of copper filled my mouth.

Someone pressed a thick cloth against my neck. I didn't even know how I'd ended up lying on the pavement. Confused shouting echoed around me, but I couldn't focus past the pain.

"You go after that bastard, I got this one!" a man yelled practically in my ear. Lower, the speaker said, "Hold on, Jack."

I tried to respond, and blood burbled out of my lips rather than words. I tried to catch a glimpse of the man hovering over me, but my eyes refused to focus. The man was a dark halo framed by the light from the streetlamps.

"No, don't speak. Hold on." The pressure on my neck increased.

The world shrank and went white. My muscles began spasming and contracting, my fingers and toes curling in on themselves, tighter and tighter. I wanted to scream, but my mouth felt odd and I had no control.

Then it was gone. I opened my eyes and sat up. Everything felt oversized, and I was wrapped in a constricting swaddle of fabric. I shook myself loose from it and stood up an all fours. Blinking, I saw my front legs that were now covered in brown and black fur and ended in paws. I looked down the length of myself to see more fur and a dog-like body that ended in a tail. I knew I should be freaking out, but it felt natural. Right.

The cop who'd been tending my wound screamed, backing away from me with wide eyes.

I WOKE UP WITH a gasp to someone shaking my shoulder. The dream world overlapped with the real world for a moment as I looked up at Jack leaning over me. Seeing me open my eyes, Jack straightened up.

"Sun's set, it's safe for you to get up now. I dug up some of the supplies we keep for visiting vampires." Jack held up a red squeeze bottle and shook it. "Sorry I couldn't get this for you last night. It took me a while to deal with Stacy, and then, since you aren't officially here as a vampire, I had to come up with an excuse to get into the blood stock."

I sat up, and as I did so I realized that I still had the amulet clutched in one hand. I squeezed my fist around it, hoping Jack hadn't spotted it. The movement made my breasts rub the blanket. I flushed, pulling the blanket up with one hand, crossing both arms across my chest and hunching my shoulders. My binder and jacket were folded over my shoes under the bed; I'd taken them off last night before laying down.

"So that's my breakfast?" I went to point, realized that to do that I'd have to drop the blanket, instead nodding my head at the bottle in Jack's hand.

"Yeah, I warmed it up for you, but I know from my coworker's complaints when he has to drink this stuff that it's not as good as fresh."

"I'm sure it's fine."

Jack sat down on the cot across from me and went to hand it to me, but hesitated, glancing at my arms and hunched shoulders. He changed his movement and set the bottle on the rickety side table instead.

"Thanks."

Jack stood and paused. "What's that?" His eyes fixed on my hand.

I tried to cover my wince and glanced down. The amulet wasn't that big, but I had small hands, and part of it was visible between my fingers. The gold must have glinted in the overhead lights and drawn Jack's attention.

"Nothing. A good luck charm." Jack looked intrigued. I needed to change the subject before he could ask anything else. "Who's Andre?" I blurted in a panic, saying the first thing that came to mind.

The blood drained from Jack's face and his eyes went white at the edges. His voice came out in a whisper. "Why do you ask?"

I got the distinct feeling I'd messed up big time. I gulped. What could I say? That I'd heard it in a dream that felt too real? No, I'd sound crazy. "I just heard it around. Maybe Dave said it?"

Jack's expression went hard and he crossed his arms. "Don't lie to me, Everett. Where. Did. You. Hear. That. Name?"

"It's going to sound crazy..." I sputtered, but Jack just kept glaring at me. I hugged my arms tighter to my chest and bowed my head so I wouldn't have to see Jack's face. "I had a dream—well, it felt more real than that. More like reliving a memory that you and Andre were shot, and then you turned into a jackal."

There was a heavy thud. I glanced back up to see that Jack had fallen heavily onto other cot. His face had gone even paler.

"That wasn't a dream, Everett." Jack wiped at his face and I realized he was crying, had begun crying silently at some point. "I don't know how you saw that, but that was my last night as an officer, and my first night as a shapeshifter."

"What?" I looked up and sat forward, leaning towards Jack. "But you weren't bitten."

"Shapeshifters are born, not made. But..." Jack held up one hand, wiping his face again with the other. "I can't—" His voice cracked and he gulped. "I can't talk about this right now. I'll give you the whole supernatural rundown later, okay?"

I sat back and nodded. I wanted to comfort Jack, but I didn't know what to say. I settled for saying, "I'm sorry to bring up painful memories like that. I thought it was just a dream."

"Not your fault." Jack stood, rubbing his palms on his jeans. "Meet me back in the waiting room after you finish your breakfast."

After Jack left, I picked up the still-warm red bottle. I squeezed a drop onto my tongue and gagged at the taste. It was nothing like the delicious liquid that had come from Jack and the other man. I choked down another swallow, wondering if it was the anti-coagulant that they added that made it taste like ass. Though I had to admit, it slaked my thirst much better than the Gatorade had, and as a bonus settled my rumbling stomach.

Once the bottle was empty, I set it on the nightstand and finished getting dressed. I wiggled into my binder and adjusted it until everything was flat and settled, then pulled the T-shirt that Jack had brought me over it. I decided to just keep the jacket over my arm. Not only was the jacket bloodstained, I hadn't felt the weather since I'd become a vampire. After making sure the amulet was tucked securely in the pocket of my jeans, I went out to greet the night.

The hallway was empty. I tried the door at the end of the hall, but it was locked, so I exited back into the waiting room. The smell of fresh coffee hit me as I entered. It smelled as good as it always had, which I was thankful for. Now that my diet was primarily blood, I wondered what things I used to love that I'd no longer like. This room was empty too, so I decided to help myself to a cup to wash out the taste of the gross stored blood.

I usually drowned my coffee in half-and-half—my former best friend Brooke had used to joke that I drank coffee-flavored milk—but this time I took a sip of it first; no reason to risk making myself sick. Besides, my taste buds had been strange since I'd become a vampire; the coffee wasn't as bitter as I remembered. In fact, I almost enjoyed it. That lukewarm blood would have tasted much better if mixed with coffee. I'd have to try that next time.

Sipping from my cup of black coffee, I left the lobby and went through the swinging doors to the reception desk. Dave sat behind the desk, talking to someone on his headset. Jack stood on this side of the counter, doing something on his phone. He waved me over.

"What's the plan tonight?" I asked as I joined him. Jack looked much better; only a slight redness around his eyes betrayed his earlier tears. I wanted to say more, but not in front of Dave.

Dave glanced up at hearing me and grimaced but didn't stop his conversation with the person on the phone.

"I'm waiting to find out." Jack sighed and put his phone away.

"Did you hear anything yet, about..." I trailed off, glancing at Dave. I wasn't sure how much Jack trusted him, since he'd wanted to lie about me being a vampire.

Jack nodded his head toward the waiting room, and we headed that way together. As we went through the swinging door, a muscular, brown-haired woman entered from the other direction carrying a file folder.

"Oh, hey Jack," she said with a wave.

"Hi, Zoe." Jack smiled at her.

"Who's this?" Zoe stopped in front of us and held out a hand to me. "Hi, nice to meet you. I'm Zoe."

"I'm Everett." I smiled at her as I shook her hand with the hand not holding the coffee cup. As I leaned close to her, I caught a musky scent that I associated with dogs.

"Zoe is a werewolf," Jack said to me. He then turned to Zoe and nodded to the file. "Catch a case this early in the night?"

"Naw, just checking up on the fox you brought in yesterday. She just told me a very interesting story about you having a fanged, red-eyed boy in the car with you. I assume that would be Everett here?"

Jack sighed. "Yeah."

"Yet you told Stacy he was a werewolf, not a vampire." Zoe crossed her arms and regarded Jack. Although she didn't look angry, merely amused.

"It's a long story, for another night," Jack said with a blush, and steered us towards the couch.

"I'll hold you to that, Jack." Zoe poured herself a cup of coffee. Over her shoulder she said, "Over drinks. Your treat."

"Of course." Jack waved at her as she left with her coffee. We sat on the couch together.

"We can talk freer now," Jack said in a low voice. "Normally Dave could hear us in here, but not while he's on the phone."

I nodded my understanding and sat down next to him, twisting my body to the side and pulling one knee up. "Shapeshifter?" I guessed. I took a sip of coffee.

"No, but..." Jack shrugged. "Everyone who works here is a supernatural of some sort, though. Dave's a mage. He likes to eavesdrop with listening spells. He's a bit of a gossip."

I hid my grin with my coffee cup and took another sip. People were people, supernatural or no. "So what are we waiting for?"

"Since I'm not officially part of the police department anymore, I can't make an official request." He nodded his head toward the reception room. "However, PCA has some contacts in the station that we can use to get information about supernaturals that are in trouble with human law.

You heard me on the phone last night, asking them to put out feelers on your case."

I nodded, then frowned. "But you were an officer. Can't you ask one of your cop buddies for info?"

"No." Jack sighed. "Officially, I died that night you saw in your dream. If my first change had happened somewhere less..." He paused, eyes flicking about as he searched for a word. "Public, with fewer witnesses, yes, I could have gone back to work the next day like nothing had happened."

I felt like a peeping tom, despite the fact that I'd had no control over the dream. "Sorry."

"Don't apologize. It certainly wasn't your fault. I didn't know vampires could pick up memories from the blood, or I would have warned you. Anyway, Dave emailed me that he got back answers, but said he'd only tell me in person. Like I said, he loves gossip and drama. So, we wait."

"What if we get called out on a job again tonight?" I said, and Jack shot me an amused look. "I mean you," I hastily amended, face heating up. I took a sip of coffee to cover my blush.

"No worries, I took today off as a personal day. No calls. Today I'm one-hundred percent committed to helping you get to the bottom of your mystery."

We had been speaking in low tones already, but I lowered my voice to a whisper so that Jack had to lean closer to hear me. "Why don't you want them to know I'm a vampire?"

"I told you—"

"I know what you told me, but that isn't the whole truth, is it?" I caught Jack's gaze and held it.

Jack frowned and sat back against the couch, leaning his head back and running both hands through his hair, and then down his face. He leaned forward again and clasped his hands on his knees, talking without looking at me.

"I don't know, just, I'm new. That incident you saw only happened a year ago. But the vampires put me on edge, they don't tell me everything." Jack's frown deepened. "And if your death is connected to anything nefarious, I want to make sure you're safe." Jack blushed at those last words.

The sudden rush of blood drew my attention to a pulsing vein on Jack's neck. I felt my fangs descend and press against my lips, so I sipped at my coffee until they withdrew back into wherever they came from. I wondered if my eyes betrayed me too. Hadn't Emily said they scared her? I really needed to find a mirror one of these times and see what I looked like with fangs out.

Dave popped his head through the swinging door. "I'm off the phone, Jack." He disappeared again.

Jack levered himself up and then offered me a hand. "Let's go get some answers."

CHAPTER 7

BANG!

I FOLLOWED JACK BACK out to the reception area. "So, Everett Boesch?" Jack asked, approaching the desk. "The guy I called about yesterday from my apartment building."

"Police were called about an attack in front of the building, and found a dead body," Dave said without looking up from his monitors, continuing to clack away on his keyboard as he talked.

I furrowed my brow. "But the attack happened outside, so why search inside?"

Dave ignored me and kept talking. "Turns out, the girl killed was the roommate of the guy you asked me about. Anyway, what I want to know is, what is your interest? Doesn't really seem like our gig."

"Like I said, that was why I was late to work yesterday, and I was curious." Jack tapped the counter and shot me a glance that I took to mean "be quiet". "Just curious, that was all."

"How the heck did this make you late? You don't even live on the floor where the body was found." Dave took his hands off the keys and spun away from his monitors to stare up at Jack. "And was this really important enough for you to come in on your day off?"

Jack gave Dave a little half-smile and slung his arm around my shoulder. I couldn't stop from blushing at the contact. "Naw, came back to pick up this one." He let go of me, but I wished he hadn't. "To give a new shapeshifter a little night out on the town. Just thought I'd get the scoop about my apartment building on the way out."

"You want to spend your free time with the newbies, fine, have fun." Dave rolled his eyes and went back to his monitors. The exit door behind us buzzed as Dave unlocked it.

"The cute ones, sure." Jack grinned and winked at me, and my embarrassment deepened. Jack went over and pulled open the door before the buzzer ended. "After you, sir."

"Thanks," I mumbled, trying to keep the stupid grin that I felt bubbling up off my face. I stepped out the door onto the porch, glad I had an excuse to hide my expression from Jack.

The crack of a gun shattered the silence of the night, and it felt like I had suddenly been punched in the chest. I gasped and fell backwards.

Blood sprayed up from my chest in an arc.

Jack caught me, a line of my blood bisecting his face.

I tried to speak, but blood burbled out of my mouth instead of words. Jack dragged me back inside, slamming the metal security door behind us.

Dave tore off his headset and rushed out from behind the reception desk. "Shit, he's been shot."

Jack laid me out on the floor and then put both hands over the wound, putting pressure on it. My chest didn't hurt, much. I'd have thought a gunshot wound would have hurt more. I felt disconnected from my body, and my limbs didn't seem to want to obey me.

My fingers twitched, and my heels drummed on the floor as I fought to move. My blood, pooling beneath me, stuck to my clothing, soaking into my shirt and khakis. I felt my fangs descend to prick my lips.

A red-headed woman burst into reception hall. Her face was so pale her red freckles stood out like marks of paint.

"Dave, activate the security perimeter," the woman snapped. "Put your headset back on and watch the cameras while Ted and Zoe hunt down the shooter."

Dave scrambled back to his chair while the red-haired woman whirled toward Jack and me. "Jack, how is he still alive? He was shot right through the heart." She fell to her knees next to Jack. "Wait, those are fangs."

Jack grimaced, glancing up at the woman. "Stacy, I might have lied about him last night. He's a vampire, not a shapeshifter. He'll be fine once he gets blood back in his system."

Stacy sighed and stood back up. Blood stained her perfect pencil skirt. "I'll go get the stock then, but you better have a good explanation for this, Jack." She turned and stormed away.

Something jumped in my pocket against my leg. That was the pocket I'd put the amulet in. Luckily Jack didn't seem to notice, too focused on keeping pressure on my gunshot wound.

My head pounded and my thoughts grew fuzzy. Still keeping pressure on my chest, Jack leaned toward me. "Just hold on, Everett. Stay with me!"

His warm face was so close, the vein on his neck pulsing with a delicious, pounding beat. I jerked my head up, snapping my teeth at the snack leaning over me. Jack pulled back quickly, as if he'd been expecting my reaction.

Dave was talking quickly to someone on his headset, but I was too out of it to make sense of what he was saying.

A few minutes later Stacy's heels came clacking back, holding another of the red plastic squeeze bottles. By now I was thrashing against Jack's weight, and Jack was doing more to try and hold me down than to put pressure on the wound. Jack was my friend, and I didn't want to eat him, but it was like I had only partial control over myself.

Stacy upended the bottle over my mouth without ceremony, and I greedily gulped it down. Like before, the blood was only lukewarm, but this time it tasted like the best thing in the world. After a moment I stopped fighting against Jack's hands. Jack let go of me and sat back.

My chest tightened, and I felt a popping sensation. A bullet clattered to the floor and I sat up, gasping for breath. I hadn't even realized I hadn't been breathing until now. I was still very thirsty, but I was back to myself enough to be able to retract my fangs.

"Are you okay?" Stacy asked, hands on her hips, her mouth a tight, thin line.

"I think so," I stammered, putting a hand to my chest to feel where I'd been shot. There was still a hole through my T-shirt and binder, and I was covered in blood, but my skin was unbroken, as if I'd never been shot.

Dave raised his voice. "Zoe and Ted found the shooter's scent, but lost him at the highway."

Stacy glanced back at Dave. "Thanks. Tell them to come back. If he got to the highway, he's gone." She turned back to me. "Now explain."

"Someone's after Everett." Jack sat back on his heels and groaned. "They don't know he's a vampire—" He picked up the smashed bullet and tossed it to Stacy, who caught it with a snap of her hand. "—yet, obviously, and I'm trying to keep it that way."

Stacy brought the bullet up to her nose and sniffed it. She made a face. "You're right. Not silver. Why not tell me, at least?"

Jack grimaced, opening and closing his mouth a few times. I glanced at Jack, and then at Stacy. She was so pale, paler even than most red-heads. Right, Jack had said she was a vampire. One of those that he didn't trust.

Finally, Jack managed to spit some words out. "I'm sorry, Stacy. He's new in town, and hasn't told anyone he's here. I don't know all the vampire rules. I didn't want him to get in trouble, but I also didn't want to give the people hunting him a chance to find out what he really is."

Stacy put her hands on her hips and glared at Jack, and then me. "Fine, I guess I can see where you were coming from. Still, he can't stay here, you understand?"

"Yes, got it." Jack nodded vigorously. "I wasn't planning for him to. I just couldn't have him spend the day at my apartment building with it crawling with cops. We were on our way out when he got shot."

The front door buzzed, and then opened. A big, black wolf came inside, accompanied by a tall, pale man that I assumed was Ted.

"I didn't smell anyone else around, and the man who shot him is long gone," the wolf said.

The wolf came up to me where I was still sitting on the floor, trying to catch my breath, and I flinched.

"It's Zoe," the wolf said. "I met you earlier." With me sitting on the floor, she loomed at least a head taller than me.

I froze, unable to react as I stared up into her amber eyes. The doggie smell was stronger than before, nearly overwhelming. I wrinkled my nose and swallowed, heart pounding. My fangs came down unbidden. Zoe leaned down to sniff at my head, and I curled my lip to show her my fangs. I don't know what had come over me, but I couldn't help but react to how close the werewolf was to me.

Zoe responded by pulling her lips back and flattening her ears. We stared silently at each other from inches away.

"You smell like blood," Zoe growled.

"You smell like a wet dog," I shot back, not breaking eye contact with her. Zoe narrowed her amber wolf eyes and let out a low growl.

"Hey." Jack grabbed the scruff of Zoe's neck and pushed her away. "Both of you, calm down. Zoe, you know better than to get close to a vampire in your wolf form."

Zoe shook her head, snapping at Jack's hand before backing away with a huff and trotting away.

Stacy shook her head and gestured to the blood-splattered floor. "Well, they think they succeeded. That'll give you time to get out of here."

"Thanks, boss." Jack stood and wiped helplessly at his bloody jeans.

"And for god's sake, you both change before you leave. Take clothes from the shapeshifter stash."

"Wow, Stacy, that's—" Jack began.

"It's coming out of your pay."

"—so generous," he finished with a grimace.

"Of course." Stacy waved a hand, heels clacking back away. She opened the door to her office and stopped to look back at Jack. "Enjoy your day off." The door closed firmly behind her.

I took the sweats and went to the bathroom to change.

As I was changing I caught sight of myself in the mirror and noticed something I hadn't yesterday. My throat had a red scar across it that hadn't been there before. I traced it with my finger and got a flash of memory. An arm grabbing me from behind, a sharp pain in my neck. I shuddered and turned my back to the mirror.

My pants looked like the sides and back had been dipped in blood, except for a perfectly round clean spot exactly around where the amulet had been in my pocket. That was... odd.

As an experiment, I set the amulet on the still-wet blood coating my binder. The amulet sucked up all the blood it touched, leaving a pristine circle in the middle of the gore.

That would have been a handy way to clean my binder, if it didn't have a giant hole though the center of the compression layer.

The amulet was magic—it had to be—but I was still reluctant to tell Jack about it. He'd want to know where I'd gotten it, and I wasn't ready to confess just yet. Jack seemed like a good guy, but I still wasn't sure how he'd react to finding out I was a thief working for the mob.

CHAPTER 8

VAMPIRES LOVE 24-HOUR WAL-MART

I SAT WITH JACK in his car, in the parking lot of his work. Jack rested his forehead against the steering wheel, arms crossed above his head. I shifted uncomfortably, keeping my arms crossed to press my chest down. At least the sweats were baggy and shapeless, so they did a good job of hiding my unbound breasts. Still, I hated having Jack see me like this.

Into the silence I asked, "I thought silver hurt werewolves, not vampires."

His voice muffled by his arms, Jack said, "Everett, I told you before, don't go looking to myths for answers. Supernaturals started a lot of those myths themselves, to try and obfuscate which ones are true. You'll get hurt if you keep that attitude up."

"Hurt." I made quotation marks with my fingers and rolled my eyes. "May I live so long."

He groaned into his steering wheel. "You really don't know why someone is trying to kill you?"

"I told you, no!" My voice rose in pitch and I paused, taking a deep breath as I worked to control my anger. It wasn't Jack's fault. It wasn't

Jack I was angry at. "No, but I guess I have an idea, at least. Who would have known to find me here?" I gestured to the dark woods surrounding the secret, hidden building.

Jack turned his head to look at me out of the corner of his eye and frowned. "You're right. Dave and Stacy knew you were there, but not who you were. I gave them a fake name." He tapped his fingers thoughtfully on the steering wheel. "The police station," Jack said, straightening up.

I shot Jack a questioning look.

"That's the only connection, the request I made through the agency to get information about the incident." His frown deepened. "Someone at the station must be keeping an eye on your file. When Dave asked our contact about you, someone passed our information on to your killer, or someone who knew them. The killer came out and staked out the building, on the off chance you were here. Then, when they saw you coming out the door, bam." He slapped one hand on the steering wheel.

"They shot me." I shuddered, remembering the odd sensation of the bullet punching through me.

"They didn't just shoot you; that was a perfect shot through your heart. An assassination if I ever saw one. Your killer is a professional."

"Wouldn't a professional have shot me in the head?"

Jack turned the key to start his car, shaking his head. "No, too easy to miss. The chest is a much bigger target. Even if the shooter misses the heart, the shot is likely to hit something important and injure, if not incapacitate or outright kill the victim, giving the shooter a chance to finish the job." I made a face.

"Yeah, but it at least gives us a place to start investigating." He backed out of the spot, then headed back down the road.

"Is that really a good idea?" I asked, watching the tunnel of trees flash by in the headlights. "Sounds a bit to me like going into the lion's den."

"We need to get some answers, and quick, before your killer figures out that you're more than human." Jack turned back into the car lot, slowly crunching down the gravel.

"About that... Wouldn't the killer have already thought I was dead?" I mused. "I don't really remember what happened, but I think they slit my throat before the vampire found me and brought me back. That seems pretty cut and dry to me."

Jack barked out a laugh as he pulled out onto Highway 30, and I shrank as I realized the dark joke I'd just made. "Yes, but they probably got suspicious when your body wasn't discovered. It's rare to survive that kind of injury, but not out of the realm of possibility. But with the gunshot, we have a small window of opportunity here. The killer isn't going to be looking for you right now, and they don't know I'm helping you yet. We go to the police station and try to get some answers."

"Does Andr— I mean, is there anyone you used to work with still work at the station that might be willing to help us?"

Jack shook his head. "I didn't work in Portland; I moved here from Maryland. I'd been reported dead, and some of the cops besides Andre saw me change, so the local supernatural community decided it was safer for me to stay dead and to relocate me across the country."

"I'm sorry. That must have been hard," I said, thinking back to my own family that had cut me out of their life when I'd come out. It still stung. One of my brothers, Michael, occasionally went behind my parents' back to talk to me and give me updates on the family. Michael was a closeted gay man, and I was the only family member he'd confided in so far. He'd been working on our parents, trying to get them to accept me in preparation for his own coming out, but last I heard, Michael hadn't had much success.

"A bit, yeah. Didn't mean to dump that on you. Anyway, they might not know who I am, but I know the lingo and procedures. But for this to work, we'll need to make one stop on the way first."

THE STOP JACK MENTIONED turned out to be the twenty-four-hour Walmart near Delta Park. When we got inside, Jack made a beeline for the men's department while I split off. He grabbed my arm before I'd made it a few steps away.

"Men's is this way," Jack said, pointing up at the hanging sign visible across the store.

"I'm too short and thin. Nothing in that department fits me. I have to shop in boys'." I tried not to glower at him. I did appreciate him treating me like just one of the guys, but I still hated how it made me feel abnormal to state out loud why I couldn't just shop with him in the men's section.

Jack gave me a half-smile, looking me over with a shake of his head.

"You are a bit pocket-sized, aren't you?"

I glared at him and hugged myself tighter. "I'll meet you at the fitting rooms in twenty."

"Promise not to eat anyone, and you have a deal."

I rolled my eyes, and Jack's hand tightened around my arm.

"I'm serious, Everett."

"Fine, I promise."

Jack nodded and let go. "Get casual clothes—dark colors—and a hoodie."

I waved him off and headed off to the boys' section. I quickly found a plain black T-shirt, jeans, and hoodie in my size. Next, I made a detour to the health section. A new trans-specific binder like my ruined one wasn't exactly something I could pick up from Walmart, but I'd improvised before in high school; a neoprene back brace from the pharmacy area could work in a pinch.

Once I met up with Jack and we changed in the fitting rooms, I wrapped the back brace around my chest and velcroed it tightly closed before putting on the shirt and hoodie. Under the T-shirt, my chest wasn't even noticeable. Before we checked out, Jack made a detour to the electronics section and picked out a cheap prepaid cell phone and minutes card.

"Just in case," he said, handing it over to me after opening it and putting in his number as a contact.

CHAPTER 9

THE POLICE STATION

"WHILE I APPRECIATE THE new clothes, I'm not sure how they are going to help us break into a police station," I said as we pulled up in front of the nondescript downtown police station. We drove past it, and Jack parked in a twenty-four-hour parking structure a block away.

It was about 1:00 am, and the streets were practically deserted. All the bars and other nightlife were farther north or east, closer to the waterfront.

"We're going to pretend to be plainclothes officers making our weekly report, but those sweats would have stood out like a sore thumb. A precinct this big, no one will know everyone. We just need to get back to a computer, find your case number, and take a look at who's had access to it. Just keep your hood up, head down, and follow my lead." Jack popped his door open and got out.

Jack had a big grin on his face and walked with a swagger to his steps that hadn't been there before. He clearly missed police work and was eager to be back in his element, even for a brief while.

As I stared at the logo etched on the door, I got an empty feeling in the pit of my stomach. I started picturing all the ways that this could go wrong, including us in jail, or shot to death by nervous cops. Breaking into a police station seemed like a big risk just to get some information.

I grabbed Jack's hand and pulled him back, my heart beating faster at this quick touch. "Wouldn't this be easier to do electronically? Just hack in, take what we need?" I whispered to him.

"Do you know how to hack?" Jack gave me a long look from underneath the shadow of his hood.

"No, and I'm guessing you don't either?"

Jack shook his head. "C'mon, it'll look suspicious if we stand here too long." He batted away my hand and opened the door. I sighed and ducked my head to tail Jack inside.

The lobby, lined with uncomfortable-looking plastic chairs, was empty. A bored-looking cop sat behind a pane of bulletproof glass at the far end, hunched over the counter reading a beat-up paperback novel.

Jack ignored the cop and headed past the desk to a door on the wall left of the glass, but the door handle didn't turn. He frowned and turned his head. I followed his gaze to the bored cop behind the glass.

We changed course and headed over to the glass. Jack rapped on it.

The cop glanced up, sighed, and put down his book to pick up a microphone. "What?" he asked. His voice crackled out through a round intercom set into the glass at about head height.

"We're here to see Detective Polly Gatou," Jack said into the intercom. He pulled a bi-fold leather wallet out of his pocket and flipped it open towards the officer for a moment before stuffing it back in his back pocket. I didn't see what was inside, but figured either he had a fake badge or was bluffing.

The officer yawned, flapped his hand to the door we'd already tried, and picked his novel back up. It seemed we were dismissed. The door buzzed as we approached it again, and this time it opened right up when Jack tugged on it.

I followed Jack into the station. The hallway was empty, although I could hear the clacking of a keyboard coming from one of the half-open doors down the hall.

"Who's Polly?" I whispered to him as we walked down the hall. Jack shushed me and ushered me farther inside. The hall opened up into a big, open room filled with lines of desks. Harried officers sat at a few of them, but they barely glanced up at the pair of us as we wove our way through.

We exited through a door at the other end into another hallway that ran left and right. A sign on the wall said "Records Room", with an arrow pointing right. Jack turned right, but to my surprise, he walked right past the records room to go into the men's restroom. Figuring he needed to use the facilities, I leaned back against the wall outside to wait for him.

Since I'd become undead, I would have thought I didn't need to use the restroom anymore, but I'd been wrong. Stupid vampires and their still semi-human biology. However, I didn't need to go right now.

Jack opened the bathroom door after a few seconds and gestured in a "come here" motion, then let the door swing shut again. Frowning, I pushed off the wall and went into the men's room after Jack. He waited for me in front of the line of sinks, his arms crossed.

"There are more officers here than I thought there'd be. We need to get to one of those computers, but since we don't have a login, we'll need one that's already logged in."

"We don't need the records room?" I asked in surprise.

"No, we don't need the paper files. We need to see what leads the cops have on your disappearance and your roommate's murder. We can do that with the electronic record."

"Why don't we get this Polly person's help?"

Jack shook his head. "No, she's the agency's contact in the precinct, and when we used her before, you ended up getting shot. Either she's double dipping, selling info to us and someone else, or she's being monitored by whoever is after you. Either reality means that we can't trust her right now. I took a risk using her name at the front desk as it was."

"So what's the plan?"

Jack eyed me. "Think you could hypnotize someone?"

"Vampires can hypnotize people?" My eyes widened in surprise. "That's so cool! So, what do I need to do?"

Jack grimaced. "I assume they can—at least, I've seen Stacy do it on uncooperative shapeshifters before—but we don't have time for you to learn. I'd hoped maybe you'd have like an instinctual idea of how to do it. Plan B then. You wait in the handicap stall. Stand up on the seat so it looks empty. I'm going to go lure in a likely subject, then you bite them."

"What? No!" I frowned and held up both my hands in a stop gesture. "You said it might be dangerous to bite people. That I could accidentally kill them. And I don't want to kill anyone! Also, I'm not sure how feeding an officer to me will help."

"Vampire fangs contain a natural sedative, to make victims more pliable."

I lowered my hands and looked at him skeptically. "Didn't seem to work on you." I paused. "Or that guy at our apartment."

"Shapeshifters are immune, and it did work on the guy at the apartment; you were just too startled by everything to notice." Jack shrugged. "And don't worry, I wouldn't let you hurt anyone. I'll stop you before you take too much."

I bit my lip. "What if he turns into a vampire, like me?"

"You really don't remember." Jack shook his head. "There's more to it than that. You don't turn from just a bite. If you did, there'd be vampires everywhere."

"Alright, fine. As long as you promise not to let me kill them."

I got into position and waited for Jack to return. It didn't seem to take long. After a short wait, Jack and another man entered, chatting animatedly. All of a sudden the talking stopped, and the line of stalls vibrated as the two men fell against them. What was Jack doing, fighting him? What happened to the plan? I was about to jump off the toilet seat and go to help Jack when one of them moaned in pleasure and I heard smacking sounds.

Really? Jack had lured my victim in here with promises of sex? I stifled a stab of jealousy, wishing I was the one being kissed by Jack. I bet Jack was a great kisser. The stalls rattled again, and there was a gasp.

"Not here," Jack said in a near whisper. "What if someone comes in? Handicap stall. End." His words were cut off. I imagined it was from the other man's mouth pressing against Jack's. Another pang of jealousy nearly made me growl, and I swallowed forcibly to stop myself.

Shuffling steps began to move in my direction, then the door to the stall I was hiding in swung open. Jack and the other man stood in the doorway, arms wrapped around each other and lips locked in a passionate embrace. My fangs descended to press into my lip. I didn't know if it was from jealousy, anger, or hunger, but it didn't matter. They came down when I needed them.

Jack pulled, then lashed out with both arms, pushing the officer backward into the stall. I didn't need any more encouragement. I leaped off the toilet, landed on his back, and buried my fangs into his neck.

The man flailed for a moment before stumbling sideways into the tiled wall, smashing my leg. I barely even noticed. The sweet nectar coming from the man's neck was so much better than the crap from the red squeeze bottles, even better than Jack. This time I was able to keep my head, unlike the first time with Jack when I'd blacked out from the ecstasy, but it was a near thing.

The officer sagged beneath me until we both lay on the floor, in a heap with me on top. The man's eyes had closed as I sucked, and he made little moans of pleasure that didn't sound much different than the ones he'd made earlier when he and Jack were kissing.

Jack grabbed my shoulder, tugging gently at it. "That's enough, Ev."

I growled at him around the flesh of the man's neck without letting go.

"If you don't stop now, I'll make you," Jack warned, bending down over us. He grabbed my chin, leaning down until our gazes met. The color of his eyes faded from dark-brown to gold, and for a moment I swore it was more animal looking out at me than man. "Everett, come back."

At first it was like a fog covered my vision, but as Jack continued to say my name, I came back to myself. I relaxed my jaw and pulled away, but I couldn't stop myself from taking one last lick at the blood that continued to slowly well from the two needle-like puncture wounds on the man's neck.

Jack helped me to sit up, propping me against the tile wall while he put a hand to the man's wrist, feeling for a pulse. He nodded to himself after a moment, then pressed a wad of paper towels up against the bite mark. I licked my lips a few times, shuddering with pleasure as the last few drops of blood I found there hit my tongue.

"Is he okay?" I asked. Jack offered me a paper towel. I took it, and used it to wipe my lips.

"He'll be fine. He'll wake up tomorrow with a hangover, unable to remember how he ended up on the bathroom floor." Jack stood, then offered a hand to lever me to my feet. "We need to hurry back to his computer though, before the system automatically locks his screen. C'mon."

"Wait." I tugged at Jack's arm, looking down at the officer lying on his stomach on the floor. His eyes were only half-closed, and he had a goofy smile on his face. "I thought you said it was a sedative, but he's still awake."

"It's a sedative, like alcohol." Jack shrugged. "I don't know much more. Vampires and shapeshifters don't tend to mingle much."

"Let me try something then." I crouched down and rolled the officer over so I could see the man's name tag. "Officer Hubbs, what is your username and password?"

Hubbs's grin widened, and he slurred out both slowly while I concentrated on memorizing them. I went to stand up when Hubbs grabbed my hand with surprising force. "That was the best time I've ever had with a guy. Can I get your phone number?"

I looked up at Jack helplessly. He just grinned at me, his eyes flashing with humor. Some help he was. I rolled my eyes and glanced back at Hubbs, who was still clinging to my hand like it was a lifeline.

"Your number? Please?" Hubbs pleaded.

"Three."

"Thanks," Hubbs sighed, and let go of my hand as his eyes slid closed.

"Very funny," I said to the smiling Jack as I passed him out of the stall.

"I thought so," Jack said, his voice bouncing with what I swore was suppressed laughter.

We walked back to the big room. The clock on the wall said 1:33 am, and the room was emptier than it had been. Jack went to a desk near the corner and sat down in front of the computer, which still showed a half-written incident report. Jack minimized it and began scrolling through the list of programs.

I stood next the chair, glancing around nervously.

"Sit down," Jack hissed. "You're being too conspicuous."

I grabbed the rolling chair from the neighboring desk and sat down next to Jack.

"Here we go," Jack murmured, clicking on the program to start it up. A little login box popped up. "Guess you had the right idea. What did he tell you? I couldn't hear him."

I patiently gave Jack the username and password Hubbs had given me. They worked, and after a quick search, he pulled up my case. Jack had been right. I was listed as missing, not dead, and was wanted for questioning as a person-of-interest in my roommate Lindsay's murder. There was no mention of the officers spotting me at the apartment, which was odd. I was sure they'd seen me in the hallway. If they had really been officers.

Jack glanced at the clock again with a grimace. "We need to hurry. This place will fill up fast after last call."

"Just print it all out and we'll take it with us," I whispered.

"Good idea." He clicked a few buttons and a printer on the wall began whirring to life. "We'll need to read it carefully, but I don't see any leads in here so far. No unusual access on the file that I can see."

"I see a lead." I tapped the screen on the names of the two officers who'd found Lindsay's body. "These officers. It says they were there for a welfare check on me when they found the body, but it was midnight. And if they're the ones that were pounding on the door, why didn't they mention seeing me in the hall? And nothing about my neighbor calling the police. My apartment was ransacked, and my neighbors are nosy. Someone would have called. Everything about this seems off."

"The police uniforms could have been a lie to get you to open the door. Let me see," Jack muttered, opening up a different program. He pulled up the two officer's profiles. "Are those the men you saw?"

I squinted at the pictures, mentally comparing it to the men I'd seen. "Yes, that's them." Odd. They hadn't lied about being cops, but why all the lies in the report?

"Alright." Jack grabbed the sticky notes from the desk and scribbled down the officer's names and home addresses. He checked the time again. "Time to go." He stood and retrieved the stack of papers from the printer. It was still going, but he shook his head when I lingered by the printer to grab the next page to come out. "This will have to be enough. Come on." He tucked the pages under his arm and began to walk purposefully back towards the door we'd first come in through.

As we got to the door, two officers entered from the back hall that led to the records room. We both glanced back to see one pointing us out to the other. "There they are. You two, stop!"

Jack quickened his steps. I followed his lead. The officers behind us broke into a run as we entered the hallway.

"Crap. Run."

We both broke into a run, footsteps behind us speeding up.

"What's going on?" A woman asked as she stepped out of the office ahead of us, the one I'd heard clacking coming from before. Her eyes widened as she caught sight of us and the officers chasing us. She was dressed in slacks and a button-down, but to my surprise she moved to block the hallway. "Hold it right there!" she yelled as we ran towards her.

Even with her arms outstretched, she couldn't cover the whole hallway. I darted to the left, and Jack right. Seeing me as the easier target, the woman lunged toward me. She grabbed my right arm, twisting it behind my back as she body-checked me into the wall. It didn't hurt, not really, but I cried out in surprise.

"Let him go!" Jack yelled. A second later there was a thud, and then I was jerked backwards a moment before the woman let go of my arm. I stumbled to the side and almost fell, but managed to catch myself in time. I whirled around to see Jack shaking his hand, knuckles red, and the woman sprawled on the floor.

The delay had given the officers who'd been chasing us time to catch up. One slowed down, his hand going to his gun, but the second one ran at Jack and tackled him from the side. They fell to the floor in a heap, the officer on top.

Groaning, the first officer snapped his gun out of the holster and looked at me, raising his gun. "Freeze!"

My eyes widened.

"Jack!" I yelled, backing away.

"Run!" Jack yelled. My eyes felt glued to the barrel of the gun pointing at me, but I managed to glance down to Jack and the officer rolling around on the floor. Jack had managed to get on top, an arm wrapped around the officer's neck in a chokehold, his knee pressing into the officer's back. With his free hand, Jack fumbled with his jacket pocket and pulled out his keys, which he tossed to me underhand.

I caught them, but didn't move. "I'm not leaving you."

The woman he'd punched sat up groaning, putting a hand to her hip where I noticed a gun holster. Doors opened all up and down the hall, heads popping out to see what all the commotion was about. I heard a buzz behind me, and glanced back to see the sleepy officer from the front desk come in. I also saw the stack of papers Jack had been holding sitting on the floor near my feet.

"Run already!" Jack yelled. "I'll catch up!"

Shaking, I bent down and scooped the papers up, clasping them to my chest before I darted down the hall toward the exit. Time seemed to slow again, and the officer between me and the door moved in slow motion as I ran past him, out the door, and into the night.

CHAPTER 10

CLUES: NONE

I DIDN'T GO DIRECTLY to the car, but instead wound a circuitous route around the streets and down alleys, circling back around towards the garage where we'd parked. I hoped that Jack would be there waiting for me, but no such luck. The garage was empty of movement, and there were no signs of Jack near his car.

Figuring I'd be safe enough in the parking structure, I decided to wait here rather than running off to look for him. We'd parked on the second floor, out of sight of anyone passing by on the sidewalk below. I unlocked Jack's door and climbed into the passenger seat to wait for him.

By now my phone said it was 2:45 am, and I alternated between checking for messages from Jack and scanning the parking lot for signs of his return. Why wasn't he back yet?

Should I go look for him? Though I wasn't sure how I could help if he was in trouble. I didn't know what I could or couldn't do as a vampire. Hell, so far I'd been wrong about nearly everything. And the powers I did have, like my vampire speed, came and went beyond my control. It was just too risky.

An hour later, I was far past worried and verging on frantic, and reconsidering my stance that it was too risky to go look for him. But at this point it had been over an hour. He could be anywhere by now.

A quick search on my phone that used up a huge amount of my limited pre-paid data told me sunrise was in less than an hour.

Shit, shit, shit.

I tried calling Jack's number, but the calls went straight to voicemail, like his phone was dead or turned off. It was getting too close to sunrise, and I didn't know what would happen if I was caught out during the day, but from the way Jack spoke, it wouldn't be pretty.

Thinking, I drummed my fingers on my leg. I couldn't stay in the parking garage all day; I'd get fried. As worried as I was, I'd have to trust Jack could look after himself. I needed to get to safety while I still had time.

I slid over the center console into the driver's seat, started the car and put it into drive, and then paused with my foot on the brake.

Where was I going? Jack's work? But then I'd have to explain why I was alone with Jack's car, and hope they let me in. Stacy, Jack's boss, hadn't seemed too happy with us before. My own apartment was out of the question; per the file, it was still sealed off as a crime scene.

I tapped my fingers on the steering wheel, and noted the rest of the keys on Jack's key ring. Well, I already knew where his apartment was, and I had the keys... Short on options and time, I figured Jack wouldn't mind. I just hoped the cops wouldn't spot me. Although, since Jack lived on a different floor, I was probably safe, even if they had left someone to guard the crime scene.

Sunrise was getting close. No choice. Jack's apartment it was. I took my foot off the brake and pulled out.

By THE TIME I got to our shared apartment building in southeast Portland, the sun was cresting the horizon, lighting up the sky in brilliant yellows and pinks. I could feel pin-pricks of pain starting along the backs of my hands and face. I parked the car a few blocks away—no time to circle looking for a closer spot—then used Jack's keys to get inside.

I ran around and closed all the blinds and curtains, then rifled through Jack's apartment, looking for a phone number for his work or boss, Stacy, but came up empty. I wasn't too surprised. He'd mentioned that the supernatural community tried to remain hidden, so it made sense that they'd keep information hard to find.

I used my phone to look up the phone number for the towing place we'd cut through to get to Jack's office, then called it. The phone rang several times before a business voicemail picked up.

"This is SuperTow. If this is an emergency call," and they listed a number. I hurriedly scribbled it down to try next, but in the meantime, I went ahead and waited for the beep to leave a message.

"Hi, this is Everett, the guy with Jack yesterday. Jack's missing. If you get this, please call me back." I gave the machine the number to my burner cell. It was a risk to give out the number, but it was one I was willing to take. Like most people, Jack didn't have a landline that I could find. Not that I would have used it. That would have given out my location, and I wasn't quite that trusting.

Next, I tried the emergency number listed in the voicemail of the towing place. The phone rang once, twice, three times. I was about to give up when a bored-sounding man answered. "This is Dave, what is your emergency?"

I recognized that bored tone. "Dave! Thank god. This is Everett." I paused, expecting some kind of response.

Nothing but silence came from the other end. Undeterred, I forged ahead. "I was there with Jack."

"Right. The cute one." I could practically hear the air quotes. "This line is for emergencies only, not for setting up dates. If Jack declined to give you his number, I can't allow—"

Shit, I had better explain fast, before Dave hung up on me. "It is an emergency," I exclaimed, cutting Dave off mid-word. Dave huffed at the interruption, but I kept talking. "Jack's missing. He disappeared. I couldn't go look for him because it was almost sunrise. I have his phone number, but he's not picking up, and I'm worried about him." I clutched the phone to my ear, nervous energy making me pace the living room as I spoke.

Dave was silent for so long that I pulled the phone away from my ear to check that the call hadn't dropped. It hadn't. Finally, Dave said, "Try his apartment, if you know where he lives."

"I'm here right now, he's not here."

There was a sigh. "Hold please." The line clicked and hold music began playing. I growled, but I couldn't do anything about it. So I paced, trying not to chew my fingernails as I waited for Dave to come back on the line. The hold music clicked off and Dave said, "I let Stacy know. We'll send out some feelers. Is there anything else?"

"Well..." I hesitated but decided to tell them, although I needed to bend the truth a little. "We were in the downtown police station right before he disappeared."

"I see." Dave sounded disapproving, but it was hard to tell without seeing his face, since I didn't know the man well. "We'll look into it."

I opened my mouth, intending to ask to be called with any updates, when the line disconnected with a click. I pulled the phone away and glared at it before turning it off and putting it away.

Sunlight was beginning to peak through the closed curtains, and I wished now that I'd paid more attention to Jack's impromptue lecture on sun-proofing when I'd first met him. Short on time, I cleared out the hall closet, wheeling the vacuum into the hall and tossing the shoes and coats onto the floor of Jack's spotless bedroom. Then I shut myself in the closet. I used a sheet from the linen closet to plug up the gap under the door. Dim light seeped in through the sides and top of the door, but I hoped my precautions would be enough.

The flaw in my plan became apparent when I tried to lie down and discovered the closet was too small. I sat up in disgust, planning to read the police file until I was more tired, before realizing that the light switch was outside in the hall.

Finally I settled with lying on my back, putting my arm behind my head as a pillow, and setting my feet against the door with my legs bent. Luckily, I was short. Any taller and I would have had to just sleep sitting against the wall.

WHEN I DID FALL asleep, I again had very vivid dreams. This time I recognized Officer Hubbs's face in the mirror as I relived his memory of a very unforgettable birthday night.

I could get used to dreams like this. Better than porn. In the dream I was Hubbs.

When I woke up in the morning, I was still basking in the afterglow. Although after the memory of living for a night as a cis-man, it made me even more keenly dysphoric than usual during my shower and when I put my binder back on. I sighed—nothing I could do about that at the moment—and began going about my day. Or night, as it were.

The last few streaks of the sunset pinks showed out the window when I peeked through the blinds. I had tried to check the time on my phone, but it was dead since in my panic, I'd forgotten to charge it. I cursed and plugged it in, waiting impatiently until the screen lit up and I could turn it back on.

My cell phone didn't have any missed calls or text messages. I tried to call Jack again, but like last night, the call went straight to voicemail. I sent Jack a text telling him to call when he got it. I didn't say where I was, suddenly suspicious. If the people after me had Jack, I didn't want to lead them right to me.

I called Dave back, who told me Jack hadn't shown up for work. My heart dropped into my stomach. I asked him to call me back if he had got word from Jack. He said he would, but I didn't quite believe hm.

Hanging up on Dave, I sighed deeply. I wanted to rush out and search for Jack, but I didn't even know where to start looking.

At a loss for what to do next, I left my phone to charge and flopped down on Jack's couch, pulling out my case file paperwork. There was so much, and I didn't know the lingo, so I was having a hard time figuring out what some of it meant. Jack could have helped, but now figuring this out was doubly important. If Jack had been taken by the same people gunning for me, I might be able to find him with the information here.

I spread the paperwork out on the coffee table and took a closer look than I had last night.

As far as I could make out, it didn't seem my disappearing act had helped my cause; they considered me the prime suspect in Lindsay's murder, and weren't looking into other leads at the moment. Which left me high and dry, and meant that we'd basically wasted our time breaking into the police station to steal this.

Groaning, I flopped back on the couch and stared up at the ceiling.

I needed clues if I was going to get a lead on the person who probably had taken Jack—the same person who'd turned me into a vampire, and was now trying to kill me.

At that thought, I sat bolt upright. Wait. I'd been assuming those last two things were related, but what if they weren't?

If the original person who'd attacked me had turned me into a vampire, which had been my original assumption, why had they subsequently tried to kill me again, but not in a way that would kill a vampire?

They'd shot me in the heart, yes, but with a regular bullet, and after a helping of blood, I'd been fine. If they'd wanted to kill a vampire they would have...what? How could a vampire be killed? Stacy had said something about silver?

I wished again that Jack was here. He'd know. All I had to go on was vampire fiction, and that had already failed me badly already with werewolves. Plus, why turn me into a vampire if they were then just going to try to kill me again the next night?

This wasn't working. Now I had even more questions than I'd started with. Frustrated, I began pacing around Jack's apartment, trying to distract myself by looking at Jack's posters. The movie posters continued into the bedroom, although the ones in here trended to the shirtless man variety, as opposed to the action movie theme from the living room.

I snooped through Jack's bedroom closet, admiring how stylish his whole wardrobe was, yet he hadn't complained about having to shop at Walmart for clothes last night. I didn't know much about fashion, but I used his Wi-Fi to look up some of the labels from the closet. Nothing fancy. Hot and frugal. Damn.

I opened up the door to the second bedroom and discovered Jack had turned it into a home office. Only one movie poster in here. Double the size of any of the others in the apartment, it hung directly opposite the desk. I don't know what I had been expecting to see, but a giant Detective Pikachu poster certainly would have not been on the list.

Snickering at the unexpected sight, I sat at the desk and stared at the poster for the movie that apparently Jack liked so much.

I wished I had a detective to help me now. I wouldn't have even complained if that detective had been a talking mouse, either. Sadly, I needed to be my own detective.

Wait, to be a good detective, I needed a journal. I rummaged through Jack's desk drawers for a notebook—all the movie detectives had one—and a pen. I opened the blank notebook and titled the top of one blank page "Assumptions". Then I wrote down everything I knew so far, and the reasoning behind it. That took up several pages and didn't really lead anywhere, but I felt better getting my thoughts down. However, it did make me more sure than ever that I was looking for two people: the person trying to kill me, and the person who'd made me a vampire.

After some thought, I added to assumptions that I thought that Lindsay's killer and my assassin were the same person.

The timeline, as far as I could make out, was that I'd been ambushed between leaving work and the bicycle cage. The assassin had cut my throat, stolen my work badge, wallet, and keys, and then dumped me. After that, a vampire had come by and brought me back a vampire. But why? I didn't know. I circled "Why" twice.

When I was done, I labeled the next page "Clues", and then stared at the blank page. I tapped it with my pen. What did I know, really? Facts, not many. I went back to the living room and brought the case file back to the office and spread the pages out across the desk.

A pop of color caught my eye in all the black-and-white: the sticky note with the officer's addresses. The ones that had lied in the police report. That was a fact. I wrote that down. Why lie unless you had a reason to? And maybe that reason was that someone told them to. A cover-up.

I also wrote my conclusion that the police were working for the people trying to kill me. Not only had the second hit on my life come after Jack asked about my case, but Jack had also disappeared at the station.

I'd let Jack's office track Polly down. In the meantime, I'd question the officers.

I stood up, new determination filling me now that I had somewhere to go. I was still worried about Jack, but I felt better now that I had a lead to follow.

CHAPTER 11

VAMPIRES, YUM

THE BUILDING WAS FAIRLY quiet; most of the residents worked nine-to-fives downtown, and went to bed early. The apartments were in a residential area, surrounded by single-family houses filled with families. I took Jack's keys, making sure to lock Jack's apartment door behind me.

I'd woken up around 8:30 pm, and it was around 10:00 pm now. At this time of night, the street was quiet, and I was alone as I strolled down the block to where I'd parked the car last night. This morning. Whatever. Vampire time was confusing.

I'd swigged down a bottle of water from Jack's fridge, but I was still thirsty. Should I go hunting before going to see the officer? Or maybe I'd come off as scarier if I stayed thirsty. I wasn't really paying attention to my surroundings as I walked, my thoughts consumed by how I should confront the officer and what I should ask.

A flash of movement in the corner of my eye was the only warning I had before something smacked into the back of my head. My chin cracked into my chest and I was thrown forward. I managed to turn the momentum into a roll, jumping up to land back on my feet. I spun to see who had hit me. Three people stood arrayed on the sidewalk in a loose semicircle, a woman flanked by two men. All three of them were very pale, and they all bared sharp fangs at me.

"Give it to us, Intruder, and then get out," the woman growled in a low alto voice. She was blonde and wearing no makeup, and wore a loose-fitting tracksuit.

"Give you what?" I asked. What was she talking about?

"It calls to us," the man on her left said.

"And you're here without permission," the man on the right growled. I lifted my eyebrows at that.

"As if I need permission." I snorted. "And I don't have anything, see?" I patted my pockets to show they were all empty. "I was already mugged a few days ago. They took my wallet, everything. I've got nothing left."

"We don't want your money. Give us the thing that calls to us," the woman said in an imperious tone, holding out her hand palm up. "Then leave this city."

"I don't have anything," I repeated. "And why should I move? I've lived in Portland for years."

"Years?" She scoffed and shook her head, making her ponytail bounce. "That's impossible. We'd have known. You came here to steal, but it belongs to us."

"What?" I yelled back, cold chills coming over me. I'd only stolen one thing lately. Lights came on in the house next to us, and all the vampires' eyes flicked to look. I took advantage of their distraction to turn tail and run for the car. Three against one. I'd played this game in high school, and knew I had no chance.

The three vampires gave chase, and caught up before I got two houses down. The first male vampire to get near me reached for me, but again it felt like time slowed down. I was easily able to dodge out of the way as I sped up, leaving him in my dust.

"Think you're the only one who can do that?" the other guy taunted from behind me.

I glanced back. I knew I was still moving with vampire speed, as Jack called it, because the other male vampire and the woman looked like they were running in slow motion, falling quickly behind us. The one behind me moved at normal speed. He tackled me from behind with a wordless cry, and we crashed to the ground together, him on top. I took advantage of my smaller size and wiggled out of his grip. I tried to crawl away, but the guy's long arms kept grabbing my legs and pulling me back.

The other two vampires continued to move towards us in slow motion while we grappled on the ground. My muscles burned, and my tongue felt like sandpaper. So thirsty. I could feel myself flagging, slowing down. I could smell fresh blood close by. So close. My fangs descended. The vampire wrestling with me had eaten recently. As I got thirstier, my sense of smell spiked. I could smell it on the other vampire's breath, and a moment later sensed the fresh blood pumping through his veins. I was so thirsty.

The bigger vampire started to overpower me, yet all I could see was the pulsing vein on his throat. I let him pull me closer, pretending to go limp. When he pulled me to his chest, I opened my mouth and lunged for his throat, biting down hard.

Delicious blood poured into my mouth. It wasn't warm, not like the blood I'd taken from Hubbs or Jack, nor did it taste good, but it was better than the microwaved blood from Jack's work and it slacked my thirst.

"Are you crazy?" the guy I was biting yelled, beating at my head with his fists.

I hardly felt the blows, which trickled off to nothing after a few moments. My euphoria grew with each drop I drank. It might not have tasted good, but it revitalized me more than even the officer's blood had. My head swirled, like a pleasant buzz after a few beers. More than revitalized. I felt better than I had in days.

Ever since I'd woken up, I'd felt like I had a low-grade flu, but now. Now I felt like I could take on the world. The guy under me screamed as I bit down harder, trying to get more of the delicious nectar which had slowed to a trickle. Distantly I heard bone cracking, felt it shatter under my bites. I felt hands trying to pry me off, but the blood pumping through me gave me more strength than them.

The blood flow stopped and I ripped and tore at his neck, hungry for more. But there was no more to be had. Snarling, I let go and sat up, licking a few stray drops off my chin.

The other two vampires stepped back, looking at me with horror. The woman covered her mouth, her eyes wide. The man's nose was crinkled up like he'd bit into something distasteful as he glanced at their limp companion, and then back at me.

I shifted to stand, and as one, both of them turned and ran. I stared at their backs as they dashed away. What had just happened? I turned and looked down at the vampire I'd bitten. His head lolled to the side, pale as a sheet. The skin of his face shrunk and cracked, aging as I watched.

I might have killed him. I tried to feel bad, but I couldn't. It had been him or me.

Maybe he'd recover after feeding. I didn't know, and I was struggling to think. My head reeled like I'd had too much alcohol. I staggered away toward the car, clutching my forehead. I needed to get out of here before those other two vampires came back for their friend.

Chapter 12

Bullet Holes are Stylish, Right?

I PULLED UP IN front of a small house belonging to one of the officers I'd seen at my apartment the other night. I'd picked it over the other one mainly because it was closer to where Jack and I lived—a house in a residential neighborhood in northeast Portland. After the fight and the drive over here, it was after 11:00 pm. All the lights in the house were out and no car was in the driveway, but it could have been in the closed garage. I sat in the car, staring up at the house.

What was I going to say? Take me to your leader? I snorted. Like that wasn't cliché at all. But I needed to know more about what was going on. I checked the note again. This officer's name was Kevin Newland.

Gathering my courage, I got out of the car and went up the walk. I knocked lightly, not wanting to wake anyone. Then, when no one answered, I pounded harder. A light flipped on upstairs, so I lowered my hand and waited. A few moments later the downstairs light came on and the front door cracked open.

The officer peered out through the crack, rubbing blurry eyes. I recognized him from both my apartment building and his employee file picture. "Can I help you?"

Instead of answering, I pushed the door into him, knocking the officer back a step. In his sleepy state, Kevin couldn't keep his balance, and he fell to his butt on the tile of the entryway. I stepped inside and closed the door behind me.

"Hey!" Kevin exclaimed, sounding more awake now.

Still riding the high from draining that vampire, I leaned down and grabbed the neck of the officer's T-shirt, which proudly displayed him a graduate of Oregon State University. Figured he was a beaver. Rivals to my school, the ducks. I still felt loyalty to my school, despite the fact that I hadn't finished my degree. A wave of anger went through me, hot and sharp.

Balling the fabric in my fists, I hoisted him into the air and slammed him against the foyer wall, as if he didn't have a foot of height and a hundred pounds on me.

"Who is trying to kill me?" I growled, getting in Kevin's face. I actually wasn't even sure he was involved; he could have lied on the report because he didn't know how to explain how I got away from him and his partner. But if he did know, I was hoping that by bluffing, that I could rattle him into telling me something.

Even though I wasn't thirsty, being this close and smelling his fear and sweat made my throat ache. I could feel my fangs trying to descend. This time I was able to clench my teeth and keep them up, but just barely. I was sure my effort gave me a truly terrible grimace.

"What?" Kevin gasped, his eyes bulging. He clawed at my hands and kicked at me, but I hardly felt the blows, and he couldn't break my iron grip. My grin widened. I could get used to this vampire thing.

Kevin's face was turning purple, so I lowered him down so that his feet touched the floor, and loosened my grip on his throat. "There have been two attempts on my life so far that I know of, three if you count my dead roommate. You know who's behind it, don't you? That's why you lied about seeing me, isn't it!"

"No, Everett. The boss sent us to protect you," Kevin gasped.

I stared at him. "Wait, by boss you mean..."

"Lady Ann. She was concerned about her favorite acquirer." I rolled my eyes at that. Worried about her amulet, more like. "But I guess we got there too late." Kevin gave me a curious look. "How'd you get out, anyway?"

I let go of Kevin and stepped back. "Jumped out the window," I muttered, trying to process this new info.

"The window? From the sixth floor? You're crazy, man." Kevin shook his head.

"Why didn't you say she sent you?"

"Would you have believed us? Besides, it's not exactly discreet to go around yelling the name of Portland's most infamous mob boss, is it?"

"True." I crossed my arms and regarded the crooked cop. "If you were there to protect me, why the guns?"

"We were a little on-edge," Kevin coughed.

I rolled my eyes. "Does the Lady know who's after me? Or why?"

Kevin shrugged and slid down the wall to sit cross-legged on the floor. "I don't know. Think she tells grunts like me things like that?" He winced and massaged his throat. "Quite a grip you've got there."

"Yeah, I'm a..." I trailed off. Jack had said the supernatural world was on a need-to-know basis. Plus, it was my one advantage over the would-be killer. Better to keep quiet about it for now. "Been working out."

Kevin looked up at me with pursed lips. "We searched your apartment, but didn't find all the goods. Figured you had it on you. Lady Ann is most excited to see the latest artifact you promised her." He held a hand out expectantly.

The artifacts stolen from my apartment were valuable, sure, but the amulet I carried had been specifically requested by Lady Ann. I didn't know how'd she'd known it was there at the museum, since it had taken me over a week of searching the badly organized depths of the storage rooms afterhours to find it.

A surge of possessiveness swept over me, and I shivered as I fought to keep from clapping a hand over the pocket that held the amulet. I hesitated, unsure of what to say. It wasn't just that it gave me leverage over her, the amulet was mine. I didn't know where the feeling came from; I didn't have any particular attachment to the gaudy gold thing. All I knew is that I would sooner cut off my own arm than hand it over to anyone.

Besides, something he said didn't sit right with me. He'd gotten there after the apartment had already been ransacked. But he'd said "didn't find all the goods", implying they'd found some. I remembered the empty baggies scattered on my floor. The goods had already been taken before the cops cornered us there.

Which meant that hadn't been the first time they'd been there that day. I backed away from the officer, feeling sick. They were the ones who'd ransacked my apartment and killed Lindsay, likely using the excuse of the welfare check to get inside. And it explained why no one had called in the ransacking: it had been done by cops. Lindsay had likely been killed after they realized she didn't know where I was.

They'd left after that, but been drawn back by the 911 call made by the neighbor I attacked. Maybe he'd been able to describe me well enough, or maybe just the address of the call had made them suspicious that I'd made the dumb mistake of going back home.

I tried to keep my realization off my face as I stared down at Kevin, trying to figure out what to do. I couldn't let him know I was onto him, but I needed to give him a message to give to Lady Ann.

Finally, I said, "I was mugged leaving the building the night I stole it." I'd had enough practice at lying lately that it came naturally, rolling right off my tongue without hesitation. Plus, it helped that everything I said was technically the truth; I was just leaving out the important part and letting Kevin come to his own conclusions.

Understanding blossomed on Kevin's face and he groaned, dropping his hand. "And you've been looking for it. You thought my partner and I might have been involved."

I nodded. "Clearly I was wrong." I turned and started walking toward the front door.

There was the scrape of a drawer opening and then Kevin said in a hard voice, "Everett, where do you think you're going? The boss would like a word with you."

Hand on the doorknob, I looked over my shoulder to see Kevin had a gun pointed at me. The drawer of the table beside the door was open, and an empty holster was visible inside.

I raised one eyebrow at the gun. "You think that scares me, after the week I've had?"

Kevin just stared down the barrel at me, eyes narrowing. He obviously wasn't going to let me go without a fight.

I concentrated on the feeling I'd gotten before of time slowing down. I hadn't done it on purpose yet, but it was worth a try. Being shot hurt, so it was not an experience I wanted to repeat. The world faded as I rushed toward Kevin. I knew it had worked because Kevin's expression changed in slow motion from confident to shocked. I slapped at Kevin's gun hand, knocking it to the side before tackling him into the wall.

A shot rang out from the gun and a window shattered. A car alarm on the street started blaring, but I barely heard the commotion as I buried my fangs in Kevin's neck. I sucked greedily, and Kevin struggled for only a moment before sagging. Clinging to his torso, I followed him to the floor.

The blood was good, but not as good as that vampire's had been. Funny, at the time I hadn't liked the taste, but now I wished I had it again. I took a few more disappointing licks, and then shoved Kevin's unresisting body away from me. Kevin sunk down, a giddy smile on his face. He didn't look as out of it as Officer Hubbs yesterday night, but he was in no condition to stop me now. And if the venom worked like Jack had described, he wouldn't remember me coming here or using vampire powers. Or he wouldn't be able to trust his memory.

He deserved to die for what he did to Lindsay, but I didn't think I could face myself if I took his life in cold blood. I already felt bad enough about hurting that vampire earlier, even though it had been self-defense.

For good measure, I took the gun from Kevin's limp hand, then snagged the holster from the foyer table. I snapped the gun back into the holster and stuffed it in my jacket pocket before leaving the house. Kevin was already sitting up, looking dazed. The car alarm was still blaring outside.

"Come back!" he called after me with a pleading note in his voice. I ignored him and kept walking.

Jack's car, parked on the street in front of the house, sported a newly shattered back passenger side window, and a bullet hole in the back seat. I looked back at Kevin's shattered front window and groaned. Just my luck that stray bullet hit Jack's car.

The lights of the car flashed in time with the alarm. Sighing, I took the fob out and clicked the alarm off before getting in. Jack was going to kill me. I just hoped he was still alive to be mad.

CHAPTER 13

NEGOTIATIONS

THE NIGHT AIR WHISTLED in through the broken back window as I drove aimlessly around northern Portland, trying to think. No use visiting Kevin's partner now; he wouldn't know anything more than Kevin had, besides the fact that Kevin had probably called to warn him by now. Dave and Stacy were hopefully checking up on the Polly angle, which left me out of clues.

Stopped at a red light, I pounded the steering wheel in frustration. It cracked under my fists. I winced, and added it to the long-and-growing-longer list of things I owed Jack.

Maybe I should have gone with Kevin to see Lady Ann. Then I snorted at the preposterousness of that, since I now suspected she was behind the attacks on me. She'd have just killed me and taken the amulet off my corpse. And it was mine.

Thinking about my next move made me glance at the dashboard to check the tank. I winced. Less than a quarter tank left. I thought about where I could find an open gas station, when I remembered my missing wallet. Shit. With no money to fill the tank, I had to hoard what I had left.

As I drove north on MLK, I spotted a closed grocery store on my right with an empty parking lot. I pulled over and parked to give myself time to think. Where should I go with the last bit of my gas?

I didn't want to leave the car alone with a broken window, so instead I just leaned the driver's side seat back and relaxed, trying to think. I felt so helpless. Jack could be hurt—or, or worse. I scrubbed tears from my eyes with my sleeve. No, I refused to believe Jack was dead. Jack was resourceful, and knew how to take care of himself. Still, my mind kept circling back to worst-case scenarios.

To distract myself from thinking anymore about Jack, I pulled out the amulet and examined it again. The hieroglyphs that circled the portrait in the center were too worn down to make out without my tools back at the museum. There were two broken-off areas on either side that made me think that it had originally been part of a necklace or other piece of jewelry. There was nothing special about it at first glance, or second for that matter. If it hadn't been for the way it had absorbed blood from my clothes, I would have said there was nothing out of the ordinary about it at all. Just another piece of jewelry looted from an Egyptian tomb.

I was still staring at it when the burner cell in my pocket began jingling with an incoming call. Only two people had this number, and I couldn't see Dave calling me back voluntarily. I sat up and about dropped the phone in my eagerness to answer.

"Are you okay?" I gasped.

A low chuckle greeted me. "Oh, I will be soon, Everett," a woman purred.

I froze, the phone pressed to my ear. "Who is this? Where's Jack?"

"Now, now, not so fast, darling. Haven't you ever heard of small talk?" The woman tisked. "But no matter. I suppose it is best to get right down to business, as they say. I am a busy woman, after all."

My stomach sunk, and I felt sick as I realized who I was speaking to. "Lady Ann. Is Jack…"

"Jack's fine. I propose a trade. Tit for tat, you know."

"Let me talk to him." I tried to keep my voice firm and even, but it still cracked at the end. I couldn't believe I was challenging a mob boss, even over the phone. My hands shook, and I was very glad that she couldn't see me.

"Proof of life for proof that you actually have my amulet in your possession," she responded coldly. I imagined her examining her perfectly manicured nails as she spoke, even though in reality I had no idea if she was the kind of person who even bothered with manicures. I'd never met her before. She worked through intermediaries.

"Fine. I'll text a photo to you at this number," I snapped. "You do the same, then call me back."

"Agreed, but I want a selfie with you in the picture." She sounded almost bored. The line went dead.

I lowered the phone and groaned, putting my head in my hands. This was a terrible idea. Even with my minimal knowledge of technology, I knew she could get my location from the metadata on any photo I sent her, while I'd learn nothing in exchange. Other than the fact that Jack was alive, a little voice said inside me. That wasn't nothing.

I held the amulet up next to my face and snapped a quick selfie, but I hesitated with my finger over the send button. No. I'd wait for her to send proof that Jack lived first. I sat staring at the phone, waiting impatiently.

After ten minutes and no response, I sent Jack's phone a text message.

"Proof of life first, then I'll send mine."

This cheap phone didn't let you know when the other party was typing, but after a moment it did check the message to show it had been read. So she'd seen it.

While I waited for a response, I got out of the car and walked around the mostly empty parking lot, trying to use up some of my restless energy. I wandered up to the dark storefront. I was walking back and forth along the front, staring at my phone, when a car came screeching around the corner onto MLK and opened fire on the parking lot.

The first bullets hit Jack's car in a spray of broken glass. I froze at first, staring in shock at the man hanging out the window of the SUV holding a machine gun. The hail of bullets cracking across the concrete towards me snapped me out of my stupor. I turned and ran for the side of the building, fumbling at my jacket pocket for the gun I'd taken from Kevin.

As I ran my phone began ringing, the default ring tone cheerfully pinging in between the pops of gunfire. Without thinking about it, I pressed answer and lifted the phone to my ear. The bullets were getting closer; I could hear them cracking into the pavement at my heels, so I used vampire speed.

"Hello?" I said into the phone. Air whistled by as I ran. "Sorry, I'm a little busy right now." I struggled to get the gun out of my pocket as I ran, ripping my pocket in the process. As I fumbled with the strap of the holster, I accidentally dropped the gun. At the speed I was going it hit hard, bounced, and skittered away along the asphalt. I left it and kept running. Not like I knew how to use it anyway.

"Is," the person on the phone said, each letter drawn out. It was like the person on the other end was talking in slow motion. I didn't recognize the voice over the roaring of the air and the gunfire, but it was a guy. In my haste, I hadn't looked at the caller ID before answering. I needed to start thinking more about what I was doing.

"That."

I ran past the end of the building towards the loading docks. I made a sharp turn to run along the back of the building, my tennis shoes sliding several feet before finding purchase. The gunfire was fading behind me, and I could hear the speaker more clearly now. I was starting to get thirsty, so I concentrated on slowing down again.

"Gunfire?" the person finally finished his sentence by the time I was a block away, the last word speeding up to normal speech by the last syllable.

"Yeah, but it's fine now. Who is this?" I said, jogging down a back alley. The shooters had to have known they'd missed, and would most likely be driving around, looking for me.

"Everett?" Jack's concerned voice came over the line. I recognized his voice now that it was quiet. Tears of relief rolled down my cheeks. "Someone's shooting at you? Are you hurt?"

I wiped my face dry, glad Jack couldn't see me. "No, I'm fine, but I don't know for how long. I'm hiding, but I don't know where to go," I whispered. The light was gone, but I could hear a car's engine circling the block. It could have been normal night traffic, or it could have been the shooters.

"Shit. Tell me what happened." Jack sounded sincere, but... Could he be working with the people trying to kill me? I didn't want to consider the possibility, but I had to.

"Jack, how'd Lady Ann get your phone?" I asked quietly, ducking my head around the edge of the doorway to check that it was clear.

"She took it off me when I was captured by her thugs. What happened? Did she text you pretending to be me?" Jack sounded worried.

It was clear, so I sprinted out of the doorway and down the alley to the corner. Which way to go? I was back on MLK; I recognized the center planting area that separated the north and southbound lanes. "No, she called me from your phone, trying to negotiate a trade for you. What happened last night? When you didn't make it back I was so worried."

"Shit." Jack said a few more choice swear words. "She was lying. I escaped from her thugs over an hour ago. She must have panicked, and tried to get you to give her whatever it was she wanted from you before you found out I escaped. Let's get you to safety, then I'll tell you the whole story. Are you on foot? I don't hear a car."

"Yeah, on foot." There was sparse traffic going by in both directions. I didn't see a black SUV like the one the shooters had been driving. I tried to think. For now I wanted—no, needed to trust that Jack was being truthful.

"Is there a car or any way for you to get away quickly?"

"Your car is parked nearby; I think it still might be drivable." The bullets had looked like they all hit the sides and trunk, but it had been hard to tell from where I'd been. I headed back towards Jack's car since I didn't have any better ideas.

"Might still be drivable?" Jack repeated in disbelief, followed by a deep sigh. "Not important right now. Focus on getting out of there safely."

The bad news was that Jack's car was riddled with bullet holes, all the windows were broken, and the windshield was cracked. The good news was that now I wouldn't have to confess about accidentally shooting out the window when I'd fed on Kevin.

I propped the phone against my shoulder to free my hands, pried the door open, and stuck the key in the ignition. The car turned over and to my surprise, actually started. "It still works. Where should I go?"

There was a muffled conversation in the background, and then Jack came back on the line. "Meet us at the 7-11 at the south end of St. John's. And throw your phone away before you leave. Dave says that she probably found you by tracking it.

"Who's us?" I asked suspiciously, trying to keep it from my voice. I wanted to trust Jack, but it was hard.

"Stacy's driving. She's going to take us somewhere safe. Now go, before they come back."

"Got it." I hung up the phone and threw it out the window before putting the car into drive and roaring away. Wind stung my eyes through the huge crack in the broken front windshield, but I squinted and dealt with it.

CHAPTER 14

UNEXPECTED CONNECTION

JACK AND STACY WAITED for me in the parking lot when I pulled up in Jack's destroyed car. Jack did a double-take, his mouth dropping open as I pulled up to park alongside them.

"What the hell happened?" Jack cried as he got out of the passenger side of a red convertible Porsche that I assumed was Stacy's. He was wearing another set of the shapeless, baggy sweats from the office rather than the clothes I had seen him in last.

"Drive-by shooting," I said, futilely pushing at the driver's-side door, which was refusing to open. "Sorry about your car."

Jack came around and grabbed the door handle, and with both of us together we managed to pry it open. I got out, and to my surprise, Jack leaned over and wrapped his arms around me. "I don't care about the car. I'm just glad you're safe."

I leaned into the hug, sniffling. "You too. I was so worried when they called me to ransom you."

Jack's arms stiffened around me. "Everett, you're bleeding. Were you shot?" Jack looked down at me in concern.

I frowned, confused. "What? No."

"The back of your leg," Jack said. "Stacy, will you take a look?" Jack turned sideways, turning me with him.

Stacy got out and walked around the front of her car to come over, her heels clacking on the pavement. She glanced down at my back and nodded. I looked down, twisting back to see. The back of my right pant leg had dried blood running down it.

"I don't feel anything," I said, staring with fascination at the blood.

"From the flush in your face, it looks like you fed well tonight, so it would have healed near instantaneously," Stacy said, looking me up and down with narrowed eyes, her lips pressed tightly together. The expression made me uneasy.

"Fed?" Jack asked with alarm. "You didn't—"

"I didn't kill anyone..." I protested automatically, and then trailed off as I realized that maybe wasn't true. I had killed that vampire, hadn't I? Or had I? I didn't know. Jack was looking at me with wide eyes. "I think. It's complicated," I said as my eyes met Stacy's. "How do you tell if a vampire is dead?"

Stacy glared at me. "What kind of a question is that? And we don't have time for this."

"What about my car?" Jack asked, eying the wreck.

"Leave it. I'll send Zoe or Ted over later with a tow truck." Stacy walked back around and got in the driver's seat of her convertible.

Jack opened the passenger side door and gestured at the back seat. The top was down, but I hesitated, glancing down at my bloody leg and then back at Stacy's immaculate car.

"Don't worry about the blood," Stacy said, glancing at me over her shoulder. "There have been far worse things on my seats."

Shrugging, I climbed over the side and into the back. Jack shut the door and vaulted over the side and into the back next to me. I gave Jack a shy smile.

"May I? Jack asked me with his hand hovering over my shoulder.

I nodded, trying to not to blush as he snaked his arm around the back of my neck. I relaxed back against him.

Stacy started the car, and the automatic top began to unfold up and over our heads as she pulled out onto the road. By the time we approached the nearest stoplight the top was up, encasing Jack and I in the tiny back seat. It was surprisingly intimate.

As she drove, I caught Stacy glaring at me in the rearview mirror. When she noticed me she didn't stop or look away, and if anything her glare deepened. I remembered what Jack had said about not trusting the vampires. I wished Jack had brought someone else with him.

"How'd you get away?" I asked Jack as Stacy wound her way through the maze of tight St. John streets, avoiding the major roads. I guessed she was trying to throw off any tail that might have followed me here from MLK Street.

Jack chuckled, his white teeth flashing in the dim light when he shot me a smile. "They were humans, and they didn't know I was a shapeshifter. When it finally got dark and they left me alone, I shifted to my jackal form and slipped right out of the ropes."

I leaned against Jack, enjoying his warmth along with the feel of his strong chest against my side, and the press of his arm around my shoulders. It made me feel safe. "I was so worried. I didn't know what to do. What did they want?"

"They asked a lot of questions about where you were and how you'd survived, but I played dumb." Jack shrugged. "You did the right thing by bugging out and not trying to play the hero. Alerting Dave and Stacy was a smart move too. Where'd you hole up during the day?"

"Your place." I bit my lip, looking down. "I hope you don't mind."

"Not at all. Like I said, good instincts. I'm impressed you managed to day-proof my place so fast with only the minimal instruction I gave you the other night."

I blushed. "I had a good teacher."

Stacy glared at us in the rearview mirror. "Try to keep your pants on in my backseat." Her tone was dry, but held an undercurrent of anger. I got the feeling she didn't like me much.

Jack laughed. "No promises, but we should change the subject. Ev, you mentioned they called you about ransoming me. What did they want?"

I warmed at the nickname. Normally I hated people trying to shorten my chosen name or make it cutesy, but for some reason I enjoyed hearing it from Jack. The question Jack was asking, however, turned my insides cold. I didn't want to reveal the amulet to a vampire after the other attack, and I doubly didn't want to admit to Jack, the former cop, that I was a thief.

"You never answered my question about vampires, Stacy," I called to the front seat in an attempt to change the subject. I could feel Jack's gaze boring into the top of my head, but I ignored it and kept my eyes on the bit of Stacy's face I could see past the headrest. "If a vampire looked like, let's say a desiccated, dried out corpse, would they be dead?"

Stacy slammed on the brakes, stopping in the middle of the road. Jack and I were thrown forward, and my seatbelt dug into my stomach for a moment before I fell back into my seat. Stacy twisted around to glare at me. "What the fuck, Everett? Of course a vampire's dead if it looks like that. Are you fucking stupid? You're a vampire, you should know these things." She huffed, giving me one last glower before straightening back up and hitting the gas again.

I crossed my arms and bit back a reply. I agreed with Jack's assessment that I needed to keep my true situation from the vampires for now, especially given that I'd killed one of the locals. I wondered if Stacy had heard about that death yet. The PCA, as the enforcers of the supernatural world, would likely get word of it eventually. I kicked myself for saying anything at all to her. Oh well, nothing to do about it now.

The rest of the ride passed in awkward silence.

Stacy pulled up to the curb in front of a nondescript house and hit a button on her dash. The automatic top began opening. Once it was all the way down, Stacy turned to glare at Jack, studiously avoiding looking at me.

"I'm only doing this for you, Jack. I didn't like it when I found out you lied for him, but I was willing to put that aside because I know how passionate you are about helping people. That was, until he put your life in danger by dragging you into his mess. It's clear by his jokes about dead vampires that he's not taking this seriously enough."

"That's not—" I protested, but Stacy kept talking over me.

"I want him gone by tomorrow night." She jerked her thumb at me. "Now both of you, get out of my car."

Jack climbed over the side of the car and offered me a hand. I took it and got out. We began walking up the sidewalk, me still clinging to the comfort of Jack's hand. Stacy peeled away before we'd taken two steps.

"Sorry," I said to Jack. "I don't mind her being mad at me, but I didn't mean to ruin your relationship with your boss."

Jack shrugged. "She'll get over it. Besides, she doesn't know that you never got shown the introductory Powerpoint presentation."

I snorted out a laugh at Jack's serious tone. "Powerpoint? Don't be... Wait, you are kidding, right?" Jack's wry smile made me cautious.

"I'm afraid not. Shapeshifting and You: Exploring Your New Body." Jack made air-quotes with his free hand as he said the name. "Got bad clip art and everything. I've never seen the vampire one, but I imagine it's similar."

"Oh. My. God." I shook my head in disbelief as we went up the steps to the door.

Jack let go of my hand so he could retrieve a key from his pocket. He unlocked the door and pushed it open. "After you, sir."

"Thanks," I said with a laugh. "What is this place anyway?" I asked, looking around the living room. The decor could have come right out of an Ikea catalog.

"A safe house, of sorts. We put newbies up here when a situation demands. Like if they have a roommate, or are having trouble adjusting and need time away." Jack closed the door behind him and flipped the lock, then went around the room, closing the blinds and curtains. "Only PCA employees know the address, plus it has light-proof rooms for vampires." Task done, Jack flopped onto the couch and patted the spot next to him.

I dragged my feet over and sat down on the other end of the couch, as far from Jack as I could get. I hugged my legs to my chest, putting my feet on the cushions—I didn't miss Jack's wince at seeing my shoes on the furniture—and rested my face on my knees.

"Is this about that vampire you mentioned to Stacy?" The couch creaked and I felt Jack's weight settle in next to me. There was a light touch on my shoulder.

"Yeah." I shuddered and leaned into Jack's touch. "I think I killed him, Jack, but it was an accident, I swear."

"I know Stacy thought it was a bad joke. I'm sorry, but I could tell you were serious. Do you feel like you can tell me what happened?" Jack moved his hand over and began rubbing my back.

Jack's tone was very even and nonjudgmental, and I found myself telling him everything, starting with realizing he was gone and ending with the hostage exchange. I left out all mentions of the amulet. In my story, the vampires demanded I leave the territory and attacked when I refused, and I said that Lady Ann wanted me in exchange for him. As I talked I felt himself relaxing more and more, until we were cuddled up together, with me leaning back against Jack's side with his arms around my waist, and his head resting on mine.

Jack hugged me close, and I heard the frown in the distressed tone of his voice even though I couldn't see his face. "How long after the phone call before the shooters showed up?"

I paused and thought about it for a moment. "Maybe ten minutes?"

"Sounds like you were on the phone with her long enough for her to trace your call's location to the nearest cell tower. But for them to get there that fast, she must have had people combing the city for you."

"You think it's Lady Ann trying to kill me." He confirmed what I'd already suspected.

"I don't know the why yet, but yes, there's a good bet that she's the one that set up the hits on you. That's also why she wanted to have you trade yourself in for me. When you hesitated to send her the selfie that was probably when she sent those thugs to kill you, thinking you'd rethought the deal. What I can't figure out is the vampire angle."

"I had some thoughts about that," I said, remembering my investigator's notebook. I sat up and pulled it out of my back pocket while Jack gave me a curious look. The pages were a little crumbled from the run and the car ride, but still legible. "Your Detective Pikachu poster gave me the idea," I said, holding up the page labeled "Clues".

"That one is in my office."

"I know. Why hide it there? What, you a closet Pokémon fan?"

Jack waved his hand. "Not important. Anyway, what do we have here?" He leaned over me to look at what I'd written. "You think the vampire turning you is a different person than whoever tried to kill you? I agree."

"But what I can't figure out is, why turn me?" I sighed.

Jack scooted away and turned to face me, putting one bent leg up on the couch.

I mirrored his pose, closing the notebook and clutching it.

"I don't know, and I don't think I can speculate. Let's ignore that for now and concentrate on the humans after you. You don't have any idea why this mobster wants you? You sound like you know her. How?"

"I don't really want to talk about her right now." I crossed my arms and turned to sit back on the couch, covering my face with the notebook.

"I'm sorry to bring up bad memories, but you heard Stacy. We only have tonight to figure this out."

I groaned, but Jack had a point. "I... work for her. Or I did. Obviously not anymore." I snorted, and imagined I could feel Jack's disappointment and disapproval, though I couldn't see his face from behind my paper shield.

"Doing what?" Jack's voice was low.

I sighed and lowered the notebook, but kept my gaze fixed on the far wall so I wouldn't have to see Jack's judgment. "I was a dual major in archeology and art history at the University of Oregon. I got a few loans, but my parents were paying for most of my education. Until I came out to them. They totally cut me off, and I ended up homeless." I let out a shaky laugh, trying to keep from crying. I thought I'd gotten over this, but talking about it still hurt.

"Geez. I'm sorry, Everett."

"At least it happened between semesters. Glad I listened to the people online in the support groups." I sighed. "I guess Lady Ann found out somehow. One of her people contacted me on my cell phone before my parents had it shut off. They set up an entry level job for me at the art museum, in the restoration department."

"And in return?" Surprisingly there was no judgment in his tone, just compassion.

"She wanted me to steal things for her. Little things, here and there, from the storeroom. She always paid me for them, on top of my wages." I twisted the notebook in my hands, curling it up into a tube.

"So she'd ask you to steal specific things?" Jack shifted over closer and put a hand over mine until I let go of the notebook with one hand, and took his hand. I didn't know why, but it made me feel better.

I shook my head. "No, she just said to use my best judgment. Her only requirements were nothing new, gold and other precious metals preferred, and to make sure they were authentic. I think that was why she hired me." I hesitated, and ran the sweaty palm of the hand Jack wasn't holding along my pants, feeling the amulet in my pocket. Jack had done nothing but help me, and I owed him the truth, no matter how much I didn't want to. "It had been that way for almost a year, until a few weeks ago."

I risked a glance at Jack, who was smiling gently at me. "What changed?"

"She wanted something specific. My contact described the amulet they wanted perfectly, even knew the lot number. But that store room is a mess. Parts of it haven't been touched in almost a hundred years, and the lot that amulet was in was from the 1920s. I couldn't find it." I shuddered, remembering the stressful phone calls I'd had with my contact. "She was getting impatient. I never dealt with her directly, but my contact was starting to threaten me, and calling me daily for updates."

Jack nodded. "I've seen this before. Those early thefts were tests, to see if you'd do what they wanted and if you could do the job without getting caught. Then, when they were sure they could trust you, they had you go after what they really wanted all along."

I frowned and ran my thumb along Jack's hand. "But why threaten me?"

"I'd guess they thought that you were holding out on them. The attempts on your life make sense, at least if we ignore the vampire angle."

I stared at Jack, the pieces coming together at last. "I get it. The mugging. The thief stole my pass card so they could get in and search the storeroom themselves."

Jack nodded. "And killing you ties up the last loose end. I'm guessing that no matter what, after this job they'd been planning to kill you."

"What?" I gasped, squeezing my eyes shut against the tears that blurred my vision. "Even if I'd given it to them like they wanted?"

"That's how these guys operate." Jack slid off the couch to crouch in front of me and took my other hand in his. "Look at me, Everett."

My head spun at the revelation I'd just been a tool—and a stupid, gullible one at that. I clutched Jack's hand as I opened my eyes, tears streaming down my cheeks. "Why hire me, if they just broke in anyway?"

"I'm guessing that they would have preferred the theft go unnoticed, but they thought you forced their hand." Jack reached up and gently wiped a tear away and then cupped my cheek with his palm for a moment before dropping it back down. "It's not your fault, Ev."

"That makes sense." I did my best to gather my swirling thoughts. Jack's presence both helped and hindered, making me feel better about being manipulated, yet at the same time making my stomach do excited flip-flops about the intimate pose. I was suddenly distinctly aware of the fact that Jack was pressed up between my thighs. I pushed the thought down, focusing on the facts about the storeroom. "With a break-in the contents of the storeroom will be audited, and the thefts discovered. But if I died—"

"Especially if they made it look natural or accidental, like a car accident..." Jack added in.

"Then they might not find out anything was missing for another decade. Or more, judging by the dust in there." I swallowed, surprised my nose wasn't running like a faucet like it usually did when I cried. A small benefit to being a vampire, I was guessing.

"Well, they might have gotten the amulet, but at least you're still alive." Jack frowned, realizing his faux pas, and hastily corrected. "Or undead, as the case may be."

I swallowed again, and reached into my pocket to finger the amulet. Jack hadn't blamed me for the thefts, so I could tell him. Should tell him the truth. Jack was giving me a curious look.

Taking a deep breath, I gathered my courage and reached into my pocket, pulling out the amulet, presenting it to Jack on the palm of my hand. "They didn't get it. I had finally found it the night that this all started. The mugger didn't find it because I had it in a hidden pocket of my coat," I said softly. "It wasn't me. This is what she really wanted in exchange for you." As I said it I realized why she'd asked me for a selfie with it: to ensure I'd have it with me, or go to where it was, and not use an old picture.

Jack stared at me, barely even glancing at the gold amulet resting in my palm.

"Like I said, I would have sold it to them, but then everything happened..." I sighed and closed my hand around it. Having it in plain sight like this was making me anxious for some reason. "I'm sorry I didn't tell you earlier. I was afraid you'd have me arrested for stealing or something."

Jack gave a relieved smile. "I'm glad you felt comfortable enough to tell me. But I meant what I said, the amulet doesn't matter. What's important is keeping you safe."

Before I could respond, Jack leaned forward and kissed me.

Chapter 15

Safe House

Surprised but excited, I closed my eyes and relaxed into the kiss. Jack was a very good kisser, lightly probing my lips with his tongue until I parted them for him. His short beard and mustache brushed my mouth and chin, sending delicious shivers down my stomach, and lower. After a few careful kisses, Jack pulled away, but as he did he gently caught my lower lip with his teeth and gave a little tug before breaking contact, which made me moan.

I opened my eyes. Jack was looking at me cautiously, his hands placed respectfully on my knees. "That was the best kiss," I breathed.

Jack smiled, his eyes sparkling. "Good. Glad I haven't lost my touch."

This made me giggle. "God, no." I stuffed the amulet back into my jeans pocket. Having it out in plain sight was making me antsy. "You make it sound like it's been a while. Are you forgetting poor Officer Hubbs so soon?"

Jack's smile widened and became a bit lopsided. "Oh, jealous, are you?" he said in a teasing tone that let me know he was joking.

"Maybe a little," I said. "Or a lot." My face burned.

"To be perfectly honest, I was jealous seeing you wrapped around Hubbs kissing his neck, even knowing you were eating him." He shifted closer to the couch to lean his face closer, pressing his chest into the insides of my thighs and moving his hands to rest on the couch on either side of my hips. "Can I kiss you again?"

"Yes." I barely got the word out before Jack pressed his lips to mine. I wasn't sure who'd moved towards whom, but the kiss made me groan with need.

When we pulled apart a bit later, I was gasping and Jack's shoulders were heaving. Jack's eyes were half-lidded and he was grinning.

"Should we move to the bedroom?" Jack asked, running his hands up my side. He paused for a moment as he hit the edges of my improvised binder, but then his hands moved again back down to rest on my hips.

I had been all set to yell, "Yes!" and damn the consequences, but that pause made me suddenly self-conscious about my chest and lack of top surgery. "I'm..." I swallowed and my voice lowered to a whisper. "Can we just keep kissing and cuddling here on the couch for now? It's been a while, and I'm not sure..."

Jack gave me an adorable half smile that made me reconsider my no, and said, "Sure. It's been a while for me too. Can I?" His hands slid under to cup my ass, and he lifted me a few millimeters.

"Oh, yeah."

I let Jack pick me up and hug me to his chest. He stood from his crouch and twisted around to sit on the couch, settling me down on his lap facing him. His erection pressed into my crotch and he squeezed my butt, making me gasp in pleasure. My underwear was already damp inside my jeans. God damn, why had I turned Jack's invitation for sex down? I craned up and kissed Jack hard.

Both of us came up for air gasping, lips swollen. Jack slid down and twisted to lay down on his back on the couch so that I rested on my chest. I don't know how long we lay there fully clothed and alternating kissing and staring into each other's eyes.

By the end, I was on my side, squeezed between the back of the couch and Jack, my head resting on my bent arm. Jack was in a similar pose, facing me. Jack's butt must have been hanging off the narrow couch, but he didn't say a word of complaint.

Jack looked at me sleepily, a contented smile on his face. He reached over with his free hand to run a finger down my cheek, then draped his hand over my shoulder. "I moved out here a year and a half ago and basically threw myself into work. I didn't want to date anyone. Guys all reminded me of Andre, and he thought I was dead. I stalked him on social media, and it broke my heart when he posted pictures of himself and his new boyfriend. You're the first guy I've looked at twice since then. Thank you for breaking me out of my funk."

"My story isn't nearly so dramatic." I smiled and put my hand on Jack's chest. "I couldn't even think of dating anyone before. I just never felt comfortable, but I didn't know what was wrong with me. I turned down a lot of guys in high school. Everyone thought I was a lesbian—hell, even me, for a while. I went on a few dates with the only out lesbian at our school, even slept with her a few times before I figured out I wasn't attracted to her that way. Once I finally came out and started transitioning, it was so chaotic with dropping out of school, moving, and hormones, that I haven't dated anyone. This has been very nice."

Jack bit his lip and gave me a lopsided smile. "No wonder you're nervous. You've never been with a guy before."

"Hey, Brooke had a strap on!" I blurted in indignation before I realized what I'd just confessed to. My face burned as Jack laughed.

"You ever try it on her?" Jack asked.

I wanted to sink through the bottom of the couch. "Once," I mumbled. "That was the only time I really enjoyed myself. And what made me start to realize I was trans."

Jack gave me a sincere grin and winked. "I'm a switch."

I stared at him, and then burst out laughing. "It's a date."

"How about we adjourn to the bedroom," Jack said, pressing a finger to my lips. "No sex, I promise." Jack sat up and slid around to sit on the middle of the couch, then turned and extended a hand to me.

I let Jack help me up and sat on the couch next to him. "I'm not tired yet. What time is it?"

Jack glanced around and then pointed to a clock on the wall in the entry way. "4:00 am. You're right, we still have time. So, what do you want to do instead?"

I sighed. "We need to come up with a plan, and, I hate to say it, but I need to see that presentation you mentioned. I don't know enough about being a vampire."

"You're wondering why those vampires ran away from you after you ate their buddy?"

I laughed. "I mean, I had just almost killed their friend. They were afraid of me."

"True. It's also a bit taboo for vampires to bite or feed on other vampires."

"Why?" I asked, remembering how strong I'd felt after. Much different than I'd felt after feeding on Jack or the officers. I ignored the reheated, bottled blood. That barely counted as food.

Jack shrugged. "Not sure. Despite the fact that we work together, the vampires and shapeshifters don't really mix much. Stacy and Ted, the other vampire on staff, take care of the vampire issues, and Zoe and I deal with the shapeshifters."

"I distinctly remember you quoting vampire law at me when we first met," I teased.

Jack waved a hand and stood. "I know the basics. But you may have a point. I think there is a computer here for guests. I can VPN in to the office and pull it up."

"Okay. Then what's the plan to deal with Lady Ann? I can't keep running forever." I ran a hand through my hair. "Because I'm starting to think the vampire thing is just a fluke. Like, maybe a vampire found me unconscious outside after the attack, and—"

Jack stopped in the hallway leading farther back in the house and turned. "What, turned you? There's not just the fact that it's highly illegal to do that without the person's permission, what's their motivation?"

"Well..."

"Think about it while I look for the computer." Jack disappeared down the hallway.

I groaned and flopped back on the couch. Jack had a point. Why? The only thing I could think was that maybe there was a vampire fighting back against Lady Ann and her mobsters. But why me? I was grateful to the unknown vampire, whoever they were, no matter their reasons, but I couldn't help but be a little suspicious of the timing.

My thoughts drifted back to the amulet that she wanted so badly. I took it out of my pocket and stared at it, turning it over in my hands. Why all the fuss over this? It was gold, and old. Priceless, true, but then so were a lot of things in the museum.

The provenience papers for the amulet had been pretty bare. It'd been donated by a rich philanthropist who liked to collect old Egyptian artifacts. The artifacts themselves had mostly been looted during the Victorian era, and thus didn't come with much information about where they'd come from. Archaeologists from that time hadn't been the best about recordkeeping. And that was the best case scenario.

If they'd been bought from the black market, it'd be next to impossible to figure out where it had really come from—not that I had the resources now to research it. I hadn't looked into it more before when I had the chance, because I figured it didn't matter.

No, that was me lying to myself. I hadn't wanted to research the artifacts I was stealing, because I wouldn't have been able to steal them if I knew how much history I was taking from the public.

"Thinking hard or hardly thinking?" Jack joked as he came back inside the living room carrying a tablet in one hand.

I offered him a wane smile. "You're right, I can't think of a reason for the vampire to have turned me. So instead I started thinking about this." I held up the amulet.

Jack sat down next to me and flipped open the tablet, folding the cover open to the back. Holding it one hand, he pointed to the amulet in my palm with his other hand. "That's easy. Negotiate with her, give her that in exchange for calling off the hits."

"No!" I yelled, recoiling away from Jack. Fangs pricked my lips, and I didn't know when they'd come down. Anger hit me, sharp and hard, and I struggled to control my expression, to keep from snarling at Jack. Inside I screamed and raged.

Jack jumped and stared at me with wide eyes. "What the hell?"

My back pressed against the arm of the couch, yet I didn't remember moving that far back. Even when I concentrated, my fangs wouldn't go back up. "I don't know," I mumbled around the fangs. The burst of initial anger was cooling, but a voice in my head was screaming at me.

"It's fine, Ev. Calm down," Jack said in a quiet voice and slowly laid the tablet on the couch on his other side. He turned to face me, moving slowly with no sudden movement.

"I'm trying." I shook, and my vision turned black at the edges. Oddly, Jack's visible skin seemed to be covered in red lines that beat in time with an unheard beat.

"Are you thirsty?" Jack asked softly, extending his hands towards me. He froze when I flinched.

I ran my tongue around my mouth. I didn't feel very thirsty. My mouth wasn't dry, and I didn't feel like I had when I was mad with thirst after I'd been shot. In fact, I felt less thirsty than I had when I'd been able to control myself around Emily in the car, even if that had been a near thing. "No," I finally said, shaking my head. "I don't know why they won't go away."

"It's okay, Everett." Jack reached out again with one hand, still moving very slowly, to touch my leg. "Do you feel possessive about the amulet?"

I nodded. "Why?"

"I think you'll feel better if you put it in your pocket," Jack said quietly.

I frowned, but did as Jack instructed. Even though it was only a thin layer of jean fabric blocking it from Jack's sight, I immediately relaxed and my fangs retracted. "Huh, it worked."

Jack smiled at me and scooted over the rest of the way to hug me. "You were right, you need a crash course. Even I've learned this year that vampires can get overly possessive over their possessions."

"Oh." I sighed and let Jack pull me back down onto the couch.

Jack pulled me up close to him and wrapped an arm around my shoulder. I cuddled up against Jack's side while he propped the tablet on his lap.

"Now, I couldn't get into work, but I asked Dave to email me recent copies of the Powerpoints." He clicked on an email with his thumb.

"Wait," I said and sat up. "How do I give Lady Ann this thing to get her to lay off me if I'm going to flip out?"

Jack laughed. "I don't know. We'll figure out how to cross that bridge when we come to it, okay?"

"Alright." I cuddled back up to Jack.

Jack clicked the email from Dave and read it out loud in disbelief. "'There isn't one for new vampires; their Maker tells them everything they need to know before the change is even made.' Well crap. At least he gave me the latest one for the shapeshifters. Want the full experience, or just the highlights?"

I looked at the clock and made a face. "Just the highlights, I guess. Don't want to be caught out. You made it sound ugly."

"I'll keep an eye out too, but sure, you don't need the details since you aren't a shapeshifter." Jack grinned and opened the Powerpoint. It didn't open right away; the PP logo rotated there as the presentation loaded.

"I guess my first question is about the memory I saw of yours. You didn't get bit, but you changed." I craned my head around to look at Jack.

"Yeah, that's always everyone's first question. That was my first question too." He bobbed his head toward the screen, which had finally finished loading, and showed a shrugging cartoon werewolf with question marks over his head. A little thought bubble came out of his head that said, "But I didn't get bit by a wolf. What gives?"

I snorted. "Woooow." I drew out the word in disbelief. Jack hadn't been kidding about how cheesy this was.

Jack tapped the screen to advance it. "Certain people are born with the capacity to shapeshift, but most never change," Jack explained, flipping quickly through a few slides that talked about genetics. "It usually manifests for the first time after a traumatic experience."

"So, I know yours..." I trailed off, not wanting to upset Jack further if I could help it. "That fox, Emily, what happened to her?"

"Single car accident on I-84." Jack shrugged. "Most stories aren't quite as dramatic as mine. Anyway, the ability tends to run in families. There are a few shifter families scattered around the world that have a 95% success rate in teaching children to shapeshift for the first time without the trigger, but most shapeshifters are having a bad day that gets worse. PCA was originally founded to help those individuals."

The next slide had graphic of a brightly shining cartoon sun with sunglasses on, hanging over a naked cartoon human hiding behind a garbage can. The text was, "You can't change or stay changed in sunlight." "This slide's pretty self-explanatory," Jack said with a shrug.

"Night only?" I asked. "Like furry vampires."

Jack lightly bopped my arm with a loose fist. "Very funny."

"Can you change in shade, or a dark basement?"

Jack lifted his hand and made a see-sawing motion. "Depends on the person, but generally no. It's a little more magic than science, like with the vampires, and our best scientists still haven't unlocked exactly why it varies from person to person, or what about the sun prevents the change."

"Or why it kills vampires?"

"Exactly. Either it's magic, or our technology just isn't at a point to be able to explain it."

A phone rang from somewhere farther in the house, interrupting Jack's speech.

"This place has a landline?" I asked in surprise.

"Yeah, so we can be sure we can reach the house no matter who is here. Excuse me, I bet that's Stacy calling to check up on us, since I lost my cell to my abductors." Jack set the tablet on the couch and got up.

I nodded while Jack went into the little kitchen that was directly off the living room. Jack picked up a cordless handset from the inside wall that wasn't visible from my angle.

"Hello?" Jack said, leaning one hip against the counter facing me with the phone pressed to his ear. "Hey, Stacy, what's up?"

There was a pause as he listened to Stacy talk. He rolled his eyes at me and mouthed "sorry". I gave him a little smile.

"Yeah, he's still here with me. He doesn't have anywhere else to go, remember?" Jack furrowed his brow and frowned deeply, glancing at me. "Dangerous? He's not—"

Stacy must have cut him off, because he abruptly stopped talking. "You're not making any sense, Stacy," he said after a moment.

Curious, I got up and drifted closer. Jack noticed and waved me over. "Look, he's right here. I'll put you on speaker, and you tell him what you just told me."

Jack pressed the speaker phone button and set the handset on the kitchen counter.

"Jack, don't— Look, he should already know this." Stacy's voice was a little distorted coming from the phone's cheap speakers, but even still I could tell she was rattled. I'd only met her twice, but she'd seemed very put together and not someone easily upset.

I frowned and glanced at Jack, then said, "I'm just going to tell her." Jack began to protest, but I held up a hand. "It's fine. Maybe as a vampire she'll have some insight that you don't."

"Tell me what?" Stacy said in a clipped tone.

I took a deep breath and blew it out. "I was changed two days ago. I don't know who turned me into a vampire. All I remember is that I was on my way home from work, and the next thing I knew, I was waking up in a dumpster covered in blood. And I was a vampire." I paused to let Stacy say something, but the line stayed silent. I waited another beat, then shrugged and forged ahead. "Actually, I wasn't sure I was a vampire until I ran into Jack on my way into our apartment building. Even then it took some convincing before I really believed him."

"You... You're only two days changed? How are you in the room with Jack without attacking him?" Stacy asked, stammering in disbelief.

I glanced at Jack and shrugged. "I'm not sure what you mean?" I asked. Jack bit his lip.

Stacy was silent for a moment. "It doesn't matter right now. The reason I called is because of what you asked me earlier, about how to tell if a vampire is dead. I just got a call to report that a vampire was murdered earlier tonight by a visiting vampire, and I put two and two together."

"Hey, that was self-defense! They attacked me," I snapped back. Despite my protestations, my stomach twisted at the confirmation that I had actually killed him.

"The witness reports say you killed him by draining him dry."

"Yeah, I was panicked so I bit him, and then..." I licked my lips as I remembered. "He was delicious. Everything happened so fast. Next thing I knew he stopped moving."

Stacy gasped and said in a near-whisper, "I thought they had to have been mistaken."

"Stacy, I don't understand what the big deal is," Jack said and glanced at me with raised eyebrows. I shrugged again, feeling as clueless as he looked. "Everett doesn't either, so fill us in. Why are you so upset?"

"He should be dead!" Stacy raised her voice. It wasn't quite a yell, but it was close. "Vampire blood is fatal to other vampires in anything more than small quantities."

"What?" Both Jack and I said at almost the same time.

"I thought you felt weird," Stacy said in a low voice, almost talking to herself. "And in the car, being so close to you was making me feel very unsettled."

"I thought you were acting odd," Jack agreed. "I've never seen you lose your temper so fast before."

A rhythmic tapping sound came through the speaker, and I pictured Stacy drumming her fingers on a table. "We need to find out who changed you without permission. Besides being a huge violation of the rules of consent, we can't have a rogue vampire in the city."

"Where would we even start looking though? Everett doesn't remember the attack, and we know nothing about this unknown vampire." Jack groaned and massaged his temples. "Plus, we still have to deal with those human assassins after him."

"How will finding the vampire who changed me help?" I asked. "I mean, I'm already a vampire, it's not like that can be undone."

"It's your bloodline," Stacy said. "There are different types of vampires. Just like shapeshifters turn into different animals, vampires tend to get different abilities depending on their maker or their maker's maker. Without knowing your bloodline, we won't know what effects your vampirism will have on you. The fact that you…" She hummed. "That's got to be a rare one. I'll have to do some research. In the meantime, Jack, I'm very disappointed that you kept this from me. You know how dangerous new vampires can be."

"People were trying to kill him, Stacy, and I suspected vampires might have been involved. Although now we're fairly sure the two events are unrelated," Jack said, squeezing his eyes shut. "And he was able to control himself. He didn't seem like a danger."

Stacy sighed audibly. "Well, I can see why you might have thought that. Okay. I'll allow him to stay at the safe house with you until we figure out what's going on. I'll look into what his bloodline might be. That should give us a clue about the possible identity of this rogue vampire. In the meantime, Everett you are not to leave the house, understand?"

"But—"

"I'll have Zoe drop off some blood stores for you today," Stacy continued as if I hadn't spoken. "Jack, you should lie low for now as well. I'll call you again after sunset."

"Got it, boss," Jack said. The line clicked off as Stacy hung up.

"That was weird," I said. My hands shook. Stacy had a very powerful presence, even over the phone. "I feel like I just got reamed out by my mother."

Jack let out a laugh as he hung the handset back on the wall-mounted base. "Yeah, she can be over-bearing at times, but it's because she cares." The phone rang again, and Jack frowned as he picked it up. "Hello?"

"Yeah, hold on." Jack pulled the phone from his ear and gave it to me.

"Hello?" I answered hesitantly.

"It's Stacy again," she said without preamble. Jack leaned closer, cocking his head to listen in. "One more thing I remembered, and I'm not sure it's important, but the witnesses stated that they felt drawn to you, and that they felt like you had something that they badly wanted. But none of them could articulate what it was or why they wanted it so badly once they were out of your presence."

"Yeah, they said something like that to me too," I said. "Is that how they found me? Cause I'd been wondering…"

"I think so," Stacy hesitated. "I felt it too, now that I think about it. But those three that attacked you, they were all younger vampires, less than a decade old. Perhaps that's why they felt it more strongly than me. The reason that I asked to speak to you privately is that I'm wondering if you might know what it was."

"Maybe." There was only one thing it could be, but I felt reluctant to tell Stacy about it. I shifted the phone to my other ear so I could trace the shape of the amulet through my jeans. A thought occurred to me: maybe that was what the rogue vampire wanted too. It could explain why a vampire might have been around me, but why change me yet not take the amulet? It had been hidden, yes, but a thorough search would have uncovered it, especially if they could feel it on me. The mugger hadn't found it because they hadn't known to look.

The line was silent for a moment, then Stacy sighed. "Everett, I realize you might have no reason to trust me, but being cagey is not going to help us find your maker. A rogue vampire is dangerous to all of us, not just you. Do you know what humans will do if they find out we exist? Because I do. It's happened in the past, and many, many supernaturals died before we were able to contain it. In this day and age, with smartphones, cameras, and the internet, if the truth gets out, they'll be no way to stop it."

I groaned. "I don't know for sure, but there's only one thing I've consistently had with me the whole time. It's..."

I hesitated again, glancing at Jack who raised an eyebrow at me, clearly understanding what I was talking about. Jack moved over next to me and squeezed my shoulder, mouthing "tell her". I closed my eyes and gathered my courage.

"It's a museum piece I stole from the storeroom the night I was mugged and then changed into a vampire," I blurted out in a rush. Silence at the other end, so I kept talking. "But it's just an old gold amulet, nothing really remarkable about it that I could see."

"I see," Stacy said after a beat. "I appreciate you telling me that, Everett. I share your puzzlement. I will look into it further. Now, I need to go if I'm going to get home before sunrise, and I suggest you turn in as well."

Again the phone call ended with an abrupt click, and I switched off the phone, turning to Jack. "I couldn't tell, was she mad, or just disappointed?"

Jack gave an amused shake of his head. "Definitely disappointed, but I feel like more of her disapproval was directed at me." He took the phone from me and hung it back up. "But she had a point there at the end. Sunrise is coming, and we need to get you downstairs. I'll make some calls today while you sleep, see if I can make contact with this mob boss and arrange to get that amulet to her."

"No!" I said, remembering the dry patch on my jeans after I was shot. "I don't... I'm starting to think we shouldn't give it to her."

Jack gave me a curious look and crossed his arms over his chest.

"I don't want there to be any more secrets between us."

"I agree," Jack said with a nod.

"I need to show you something."

"Okay, but make it quick." Jack cast a meaningful glance at the clock on the microwave oven.

How could I demonstrate? I cast about the kitchen. There. I grabbed a decorative towel that hung from the handle of the oven and spread it on the counter, then grabbed a knife from the knife block. Jack frowned, but didn't say anything as I held my left arm out over the towel and pressed the knife to the back of my forearm. Blood welled up from the shallow cut to drip down my arm. The cut healed over before more than a few drops had stained the towel, but I figured that would be enough for this demonstration.

"See my blood there?" I asked, adding to the spot by using the towel to wipe my blood from the knife and my arm before laying it back down flat on the counter.

"Yeah, you bleed when you're cut. Big deal," Jack said with a raise of his eyebrows.

"Now, watch." I got the amulet out of my pocket and laid it on top of the bloody spot. The blood rolled towards the amulet and vanished. It was like watching a time-lapse video of a spill in reverse. I picked the amulet back up, and the towel looked as pristine as it had when I'd first laid it down. I turned to Jack expectantly. "Well?"

Jack was staring at the clean towel in shock. "That was unexpected," he finally said.

"What do you think we should do about it?" I asked as the silence lengthened. "I don't feel right giving this to a mob boss, even if I could get over my possessiveness."

Jack groaned and scrubbed his face. "God, this is a mess. Honestly? I don't know. Give me some time to think it over. I'm exhausted. I didn't get much sleep yesterday, what with being held captive all day, and I'm sure you're feeling the coming sun."

I sighed, but acknowledged that I'd dropped this all on Jack rather suddenly.

"Alright." I put the amulet away.

I wished I'd had time to ask Stacy more questions. For instance, my T shot was coming due, but did I still need it as a vampire? When I'd been human, missing a dose once and a while wasn't a huge issue, so I decided it wasn't urgent enough to risk Stacy's ire by asking Jack to call her back.

"This way. I'll get you set up, then I need to crash myself." Jack crossed the kitchen and opened a door to reveal a dark staircase leading down to the basement.

"I'm actually not that tired. Can I take the tablet with me, for entertainment?" I pointed back to the living room where the tablet lay abandoned on the couch.

"Sure." Jack shrugged, hiding a yawn. "Just be smart, don't contact anyone from your old life. You know that mobster will be monitoring everyone you might know on the off chance of finding you."

"No problem." I shuddered. "The memory of being shot through the heart is still very fresh."

Jack showed me around the basement. The whole bottom floor had been light-proofed for vampire guests, and included two small bedrooms, a little mini living room with television and DVD player, and a small bathroom with the most cramped shower stall I had ever seen.

After Jack went back upstairs, wishing me good night as he left—which I found just a touch ironic—I settled down with the tablet on the bed. I half wished Jack had stayed to cuddle, but I didn't blame him for wanting his own bed that didn't come with the threat of possibly waking up with a vampire sucking on his neck.

Jack's reaction to my demonstration with the amulet told me that I needed to find out more about where it had come from. I knew it was ancient Egyptian, likely from early in the dynasties from what I could make out of the hieroglyphs. However, without access to the museum's paid academic research databases, I wasn't finding much more than I already knew. It was unusual that the amulet depicted a human face, since most jewelry from the dynasties featured animals or animal-headed deities, but search engines and the free databases weren't very reliable.

The rich industrialist who'd donated the piece had been a social recluse, so the information available about him in the Portland histories that I could find online was sparse and far between. Another dead end. I might have more luck with a local historical museum.

If only I could just use the systems at the museum. Or ask my boss. I sat up on the bed. That was an idea. But then I slumped back down. Jack had been right. Lady Ann knew where I worked—she'd gotten me the job, after all—which meant she had pull with someone at the museum. Anyone I knew there would be monitored. Even email was a risk. She'd found me fast enough from just a phone call, and an email would have an IP address of origin attached to it that could be traced back to the house.

Sighing, I put the tablet aside and got ready for bed, chewing over the problem.

CHAPTER 16

ARMED AND DANGEROUS

I KNEW BY NOW what would happen as I dreamed, so when I opened my eyes to find myself somewhere else surrounded by strangers, I wasn't too surprised. A pretty blonde woman who I judged to be in her late thirties, wearing a stylish business suit and high heels, stalked back and forth in front of me. I couldn't turn my head, but out of the corner of my eye I recognized the person standing next to me as the other officer from my apartment: Kevin's partner.

The woman stopped her pacing in front of me and regarded me with narrowed eyes and crossed arms. "What do you mean he was spotted at the police station?"

"I got a ping that someone accessed the file from the bullpen downtown. I called a contact in the building, and that's the description they gave me," I said in a deep, male voice.

"That's not possible. Fredo said he'd shot him through the heart. He's dead," the woman snapped. Her face was twisted up in a scowl so deep it was cracking her expertly applied makeup.

I mentally facepalmed. A disguise might have been a good idea. Too late now.

"I don't know what else to tell you, Lady Ann." I shrugged and put my hands out in a placating gesture. "My contact is on his way to round them up. You can ask him yourself once they bring them in."

"'Them'? He isn't alone?" Lady Ann's scowl turned to puzzlement.

"No, he's got some Indian guy with him. I told my contact to scoop them both up."

"Interesting he has allies I didn't know about." Lady Ann tapped her foot. "I've been keeping close tabs on him. I wonder..."

I exchanged a long glance with Kevin's partner as Lady Ann stalked over to her desk and opened an old book that sat on top. The pages were stiff and yellowed with age. She was muttering, mostly to herself, but loud enough I could hear it.

"First Rom, now Fredo. I trust them both. They wouldn't have lied to me. Perhaps he used it?" She flipped carefully through the book's pages until she found what she was looking for, then ran a finger down the page and tapped something I couldn't see. She opened a day-planner and compared it to the page. "Impossible. The new moon isn't for a few more days..."

My cell phone pinged. I looked at Lady Ann, still muttering to herself while looking at the book and the planner. "Ma'am? It might be my contact." "Go ahead," she said without looking up.

I pulled the phone out of my back pocket and turned it on to see a text message. I read it out loud to the room. "Everett escaped, but they got the guy he was with. They're bringing him to the warehouse."

"Hmm. Could be worse." Lady Ann closed the book and grabbed the day planner. "Maybe he can answer a few of my questions."

I WOKE UP TO the buzz of an alarm. I'd set it for an hour before sunset, so I'd have time to shower and freshen up before seeing Jack. I shook off the weird memory of Kevin's and got up. All and all, I preferred Hubbs's orgies to Kevin's intrigue.

At least I knew what Lady Ann looked like now, though I wasn't sure how I could make use of that information.

The shower stall proved to be as tight as it had looked on initial inspection. I was not a big guy; I'd even been referred to a few times when I'd passed in the gay bars as a "twink", which simultaneously sent thrills of joy through me and pissed me off. It wasn't like I could help being short. Yet my shoulders almost brushed the sides of the shower. Sadly I didn't have any other clothes to change into, so I had put back on the dirty T-shirt and bullet-hole-filled, blood-stained pants that I'd worn the day before.

Once I was ready, I climbed the basement stairs to the kitchen door, but the door was locked. I knocked on it, but no one answered. I waited for a bit and knocked again. Still no answer, so I went back downstairs and flopped on the couch.

Bored, I turned on the TV using the remote I found on the side table. It showed an ad for a moment before cutting back to two news announcers.

The woman announcer smiled and began speaking. "Welcome back to KATU Evening News. In local news, Portland residents are urged to keep their eyes out for Everett Boesch, who is wanted by police in the murder of her roommate, Lindsay Spakes."

I cringed and leaned forward, both repulsed and curious about what else they had to say.

The camera moved to focus on the male newscaster, and my picture appeared to the side. It was the one taken by the museum for my work badge, so not only did the yellowish lighting make my skin look sallow, it was from before I started hormones. I winced.

The newscaster began speaking. "Citizens are urged to call 911 to report sightings of this individual, who police say is armed and dangerous. In addition to attacking an officer at his home last night, Everett is also suspected of stealing several valuable pieces from the Portland Art Museum. Everett Boesch, also known as—"

I flipped the TV off in disgust, then leaned forward, putting my head between my knees and wrapping my hands around the back my head. My breathing became shallower and I felt like crying. I recognized the start of a panic attack.

Not only was I being accused of murder, but I'd just been deadnamed on local TV. I wasn't out as trans to many people, especially since I'd been able to pass fairly well before hormones, at least until I opened my mouth.

And hormones had taken care of that problem.

Although I supposed as a vampire, my old life had already been lost.

As the initial burst of dread and panic wore off, I started to realize I didn't really have much in my old life that I would regret losing. I'd already lost my best friend and my family when I'd come out.

That sent a renewed burst of panic through me that sent me bolting straight up. God, what if my parents saw this? They were going to think I was a thief and a murderer. Well, I was a thief, but it wasn't like I wanted my parents to know that. In fact, I'd been hoping that after a while they'd cool off, and we could reconnect, but that wouldn't happen if they believed the news report.

In the silence, the creaking of the floor above could be heard clearly. I jumped to my feet and scrambled back up the stairs to pound on the locked door. "Jack! Jack!"

Jack's shoes squeaked on the linoleum as he came over to the door.

"Everett? What's the big emergency?" His voice was muffled, but audible.

"The door's locked!" I jiggled the knob for emphasis.

"Yeah, because it's not safe for you to come out yet. Give it another fifteen for the sun to finish setting while I put these groceries away, then I'll unlock it." His shoes squeaked as he retreated for a few steps before coming back. "Oh, and Zoe dropped by some food for you too. I'll warm one up and send it down in the dumbwaiter. I'd feel better if you drank it before you came up."

"Dumbwaiter?" I repeated, thinking I'd misheard.

"Yeah, you know, it's a little elevator for sending food and drink up and down floors. I think the door is next to the couch down there." Jack's voice faded, and a moment later I could hear him rummaging around in the kitchen.

I stomped back down the stairs and looked around. There was a small, square, wooden door set into the wall. I'd opened it last night before bed while exploring the apartment, and just figured it was an empty cupboard.

Rather than sitting back down on the couch to wait, I paced the living room, trying to think. I needed to get a message to my family, explain what happened, that I wasn't a murderer. But how?

I sat on the couch and turned on the tablet. A quick internet search on how to send anonymous emails directed me to a helpful website that would send the message on my behalf, so it wouldn't reveal my IP address if Lady Ann's IT thugs intercepted it. Perfect.

I couldn't remember my mom's email address, so I flipped over to another tab and signed in to my online email client. I figured that would be safe enough. I hadn't been able to check my email in days, and my account showed over two-hundred unread messages. I was going to ignore them, but the subject line of one of the newest emails caught my attention.

"EVERETT, PENDANT TONIGHT OR PARENTS DIE", received just fifteen minutes ago.

"Shit, well, that's straight to the point," I muttered to myself as I flipped back to the anonymous email website and deleted most of what I'd already written into the message body box.

There was a rattling noise and then the cupboard dinged helpfully. At almost the same time Jack yelled, so muffled I barely heard it, "Dinner!"

I rolled my eyes and tapped out a new message to my mom. "Mom, this is Everett. I didn't kill anyone, and you and Dad are in danger. Get somewhere safe, NOT the police. They can't be trusted. Love you. Everett."

I hit send before I could overthink it and then closed the tab. I left my email open for now so I could show Jack the threat.

I opened the dumbwaiter door to find a microwaved bottle of steaming blood—ick—and, praise Jack's name to the heavens, a new set of clothes in my size. I choked down the blood before changing into the fresh clothes. They were just cheap Walmart brands, but tasteful. The shirt was button-up in a color that went with my lighter skin tone, and the jeans had a simple, straight leg.

I heard the click of the lock disengaging as I finished dressing. I grabbed the tablet and the empty bottle, then jogged up the stairs and burst into the kitchen.

Jack sat at the kitchen table, about to take the first bite of a freshly made sandwich. He set it down without taking a bite and gave me an amused look as I pulled out a chair and sat down across from him.

"Early bird gets the worm is not a motto for vampires to live by. Sunset is no joke. Get the timing wrong and you're toast." Jack picked his sandwich back up and took a big bite.

"You need to see this." I set the empty bottle aside so I could turn on the tablet, then flipped it around to show Jack the threatening email.

Jack finished chewing and swallowing while he glanced at the screen, then he sighed. "You weren't supposed to get into your email, Everett. No contact, remember?"

"I didn't send anything from it!" I protested, lowering the tablet to lay flat on the table. "I thought it would be okay to at least look at it. She's going after my parents, Jack."

Jack sighed again and let go of one side of his sandwich to put a hand over mine. "She's just trying to flush you out, Ev. If you don't try to contact them, she'll leave them alone. No reason to get her hands dirty if she doesn't have to." He pulled his hand away and went back to eating.

I chewed on my lower lip, letting Jack eat in silence. I thought watching Jack eat would make me hungry. After all, I hadn't had anything to eat but blood for days, but strangely, while watching Jack did make me want food, the smell of the turkey and cheese from the sandwich wasn't appealing at all, and actually made me wrinkle my nose. I fiddled with the tablet, trying to ignore the smell, and impatiently waiting for Jack to finish eating.

As he ate, Jack kept glancing at me, his frown deepening between each bite. When he finished, he pushed the plate away and laced his hands together on the table, giving me a hard look.

"You tried to contact them, didn't you?"

"I needed to warn them! I sent it through an anonymous web service, so it didn't come from my email. She can't use it to trace back to my location, so it's fine, right?"

I cringed at Jack's narrowed eyes and deepening frown as I blurted out my confession.

"No contact means no contact!" Jack yelled. He pushed back from the table so hard his chair almost fell over, stomped a few paces away, then turned his back on me with his fists clenched at his side. He blew out a deep breath and turned back around, crossing his arms. "Everett, sending the warning, even anonymously, means that you saw the threat and it got to you. If you didn't respond, she wouldn't know if you even saw the email, and that if she killed them, she'd lose potential leverage over you later. It doesn't matter if she can trace it back to you. Now all she has to do is stake out your parents and kill you when you show up."

I frowned. "So I just don't show up."

Jack shook his head. "Then she'll kill them. If she doesn't now that you've acknowledged the threat, she'll lose face. Let me see the email again.

Is there a time limit?"

I brought the email back up. "Yeah, 2:00 am."

Jack took the tablet from me and clicked on the screen, growing thoughtful. "This was sent just after sunset. And the time limit... Vampire hours." He scrolled back through my unread messages. "Look, here. She sent you other messages over the last few days, mostly during the day. But tonight, she waited until dark. Did she somehow figure out you're a vampire now?" He was speaking low, mostly to himself, but I decided to respond as if he'd asked me the question.

"I don't know how she would have. I doubt she's part of the supernatural community."

"True. If she knew about the supernatural world, I wouldn't have been able to escape from her thugs the way I did. Still." Jack shook his head and closed my email. "It's suspicious."

I shrugged, but my hands were shaking. I clasped them together and put them in my lap. "What do we do now then?"

"First, we don't panic. I'm going to make a few calls, see what we can do from here." Jack grabbed the phone handset. "C'mon, let's go to the living room. Better seating."

I stayed sitting where I was, trying to hold back tears. I could tell it was time for my T shot by how emotional I was getting.

Jack came back and crouched down next to me. "I shouldn't have yelled, I'm sorry. I should have been more explicit in my instructions and explained why no contact was so important."

"It's okay," I mumbled. "I should have known better. Seeing myself all over the news and then the email, I panicked."

"News?" Jack frowned.

"When I first found the door locked, I was bored. I turned on the TV, and the news was on. They were all but calling me a murderer, and then they outed me, misgendered me, and deadnamed me." Remembering this the dam burst, and I couldn't hold back the tears anymore.

"Goddess damn it," Jack muttered and leaned forward to wrap me in a hug, letting me sob into his shoulder. "Yeah, I can see why you were on edge. I'm betting that was part of her plan to flush you out."

"Well, it's working." Feeling a little better now, I sat back and dabbed at my eyes with my shirt collar.

"She's had a while to study you. To have contacted you that quickly after you had to drop out of school... She's had her eye on you for a while. Longer than you'd think. She'll know all the right places to apply pressure, like with your roommate." Jack rocked back to his feet and then offered a hand to me.

I took it, and allowed Jack to pull me up and lead me into the living room. "But why go after my parents? We're estranged. I haven't talked to them since the day I came out," I protested as we sat down together on the sofa.

Jack gave me a patient smile. "Have you tried to contact them since then?"

"Of course! My brother, Michael, he works at Dad's shop. I talk to him fairly often, ask him to pass on messages. But they never call me back."

Jack made a finger-gun and pointed it at me. "Bang. She's got you. She knew you'd care if she threatened them because of those calls."

"How'd she..." I paused. Mobster. Crime boss. "She had my phones tapped?"

"That'd be my guess," Jack agreed, lifting the handset. "Now, what city do they live in? I'm going to ask the office to do a welfare check."

"Hood River." I gave Jack their address and phone numbers from memory. "But do you think it's a good idea to call Stacy for help?"

"It's dangerous for you to leave the house." Jack finished dialing and lifted the phone to his ear.

"Do you have to tell Stacy what I did?" I pleaded with him while the phone rang. "I'm already embarrassed enough about it. We'll just pop out there and make sure they're safe, and Stacy will never have to know."

"You know I can't do that, Everett," Jack said, putting a hand over the receiver. "Her voicemail just came on; she must not have gotten to the office yet. I'll leave a message, and she'll call us back when she gets in."

STACY CALLED BACK ABOUT fifteen minutes later. Jack answered and put the handset on speakerphone mode.

"Hi, Jack. I got your message." Stacy's tone was sharp. I bolted upright. "Then, you can send someone to—"

"No," Stacy cut me off. "This is a human matter. We can't get involved."

"Can't or won't?" I growled, leaning down close to the speaker. "It's my parents!"

"Fine, won't. Your parents, who are still human, are being threatened by a human. Therefore, this is a human matter." I tried to speak again, and Stacy talked over me. "You didn't go through the normal process for new vampires, so I wouldn't expect you to know this, and perhaps Jack didn't know this either, still being relatively new to the community, but before a human is allowed to become a vampire they are expected to fake their death and then cut all ties with their old human life."

"What?" I sank back into the couch, stunned, and glanced at Jack, who looked just as confused. "But why?"

"This is exactly the reason. You are tempted to use your newfound abilities to run to your parents' rescue, I can hear it in your voice, but what happens then? Someone sees you and word gets out about us."

"That doesn't make any sense," Jack said, shaking his head. "Obviously my circumstances are different. I'd been reported shot in the throat in full view of witnesses, but normally shapeshifters can go right back to their human life like nothing happened."

Stacy's tone softened. "But you age only slightly slower than normal humans. How would you feel if you had to watch your loved ones fade away and die of old age while you remain the same? Trust me, it's easier this way."

I frowned. Living forever hadn't even occurred to me yet since I was just trying to just survive till tomorrow. I shifted uncomfortably. "So I'm just supposed to let them die?" I whispered in disbelief. I felt numb. I'd always thought that they'd come around and I'd reconcile with them. That couldn't happen if they were dead.

Jack slipped an arm around my shoulder and hugged me close, offering silent comfort.

"But, the person after them is the same person after me," I said, trying another tack. "Doesn't that make it a matter for supernaturals?"

"You know this for certain?" Stacy asked.

"Who else would it be?" My voice raised at the end and I sat forward. I knew I was starting to panic. I even felt my fangs trying to come down. Jack tugged me back down and I closed my eyes, silently counting to ten while doing deep breathing exercises to calm myself. Meanwhile, Jack began gently rubbing my shoulders.

Stacy's sigh was audible over the speaker. "Jack, Everett sounds a little on edge. Any worries he'll attack you?"

"No, he's fine. His fangs came down, but he caught himself." Jack sounded relaxed and jovial, but I noticed he didn't stop rubbing.

"I still can't believe he is less than a week changed," Stacy said. "Now, as to the matter at hand of the person or persons after you, Jack's earlier voicemail explained the situation. I'll bring the matter up to the council on what is to be done about your unique situation. This matter is urgent enough that I've scheduled an emergency council meeting for tomorrow night—"

"Tomorrow?" I yelled, appalled. By then it would be too late for my parents. Jack pulled his hands back and frowned at the phone.

"Do not cut me off. The council members are busy people. You're lucky it is happening so quickly. What is that modern expression?" She paused and I could hear a pencil tapping. "Ah, yes, beggars can't be choosers. In the meantime, you are safe enough where you are for the moment, so just sit tight."

"But—"

Stacy tutted, her voice hard as steel. "Do you think I like being down a staff member for another two nights? Jack has to stay in hiding too until this has been resolved, since you've already managed to involve him in this madness by getting him kidnapped."

The line went dead. I reached over and turned off the handset, then rested my head in my hands with a groan.

"How did you do it?" I asked Jack without looking up. "Leave behind everything and start over?"

Jack sighed, and he sat near enough that I could feel him fidgeting. "I'm still not sure. I don't know if it helps or hurts that I regularly get on social media to look at updates of their lives. I'm probably not the best person to talk to about letting go. They think I'm dead, better to keep it that way."

"What would you do, in my situation then? If you knew that they were in mortal danger, but were told not to do anything about it?" I finally lifted my head and glanced sideways up at Jack. He looked lost and sad.

Jack stared down at me in silence for a long moment, then turned away and crossed his arms over his chest. "I wouldn't do anything." His voice was tight and his shoulders tensed as he talked. "I'd let them go. Mourn them."

"Would you? Really? You wouldn't try to save them?" I sat up, focusing on Jack's profile and the clench of his jaw.

"No." The muscle on his jaw jumped. He was lying. "It would hurt too much to see them knowing I'd have to disappear on them again. You should listen to Stacy, she knows what she's talking about. Even if you do save them, once things settle you'll have to fake your death and never see them again anyway."

"I'd rather have them alive and thinking I'm dead than have them dead."

"That's a little selfish, don't you think?" Jack turned back to face me, eyes bright with unshed tears. His arms were still tightly crossed.

I narrowed my eyes at Jack and crossed my own arms defensively.

"Selfish? How do you figure that?"

"You're okay with them alive and mourning you, but you aren't willing to be the one alive and mourning them!" Jack yelled. He uncrossed his arms and stood, walking a few steps away, fists clenching and unclenching at his sides, then he whirled back. "You want to have your cake and eat it too. I've had to watch from afar as grief drove my father back into alcoholism and broke up my parent's marriage. My faked death tore my family apart. You think your death won't do the same to your family? Yes, it's a sham, but they don't know that."

I rocked back, feeling as though I'd been punched. I jumped to my feet, feeling flush with anger, and yelled back, "Of course my death won't tear my family apart. They've been pretending I've been dead for most of this last year already. Not going to make much difference if there is a coffin and a headstone now to make it official!"

"So why do you want to save them so badly?" Jack asked, his voice so quiet I barely heard him.

I stammered, not sure how to put my complicated feelings into words. My shoulders slumped and I felt as if I were deflating. I hugged myself and turned my back on Jack, trying not to cry. "I don't know. I guess I don't want them to die with us still estranged like this."

Jack sighed and wrapped me in a hug from behind, resting his cheek on the side of my head. His solid presence helped me to center myself and I closed my eyes, choking back my tears.

"Alright, I'll help you." Jack said it so quietly I thought I'd misheard.

"You, what?"

His breath tickled my ear. "I'll help you warn them. But—" He held up a hand as I broke free of his embrace and turned to face him with wide eyes. "—only what we can do without leaving the house. It's too risky to be on the streets of Portland for you right now, especially since it seems your would-be killers might know about your little secret."

"Thank you," I said. "I just hope it's enough to save them!"

CHAPTER 17

YOU CAN'T SAVE EVERYONE

I PACED WHILE JACK sat back down on the couch. "So, what's the plan then?"

"Let's try the easiest route first: calling them." Jack pulled a new prepaid cellphone out of his pocket and then looked expectantly at me. "And come sit down. You're making me nervous with all that pacing."

"Won't she be tracing any calls that come into their number?" I asked, whirling to face Jack.

"Probably, but tracing takes time. We'll start a timer, no longer than thirty seconds on the phone, then I hang up no matter what." Jack patted the couch cushion next to him, and I came over and sat on the edge. My leg jumped, and I tapped my foot. I wanted to move, go somewhere, do something, and was having a hard time sitting still.

Jack put the phone to his ear, listening to it ring. After a moment he put it down again. "No answer. Do you have any other way to reach them?"

"That was their house phone. They both have cellphones." I gave him my mom's number first.

"No answer."

"Try my dad's cell."

I stared at Jack impatiently, groaning when he again lowered the phone without saying anything.

"Nothing?" My panic was returning. "Why aren't they answering?" My voice raised and cracked at the end. I was sure I sounded like a teenager, but I was too panicked to be embarrassed.

"You have no idea at all where they could be?" Jack looked at me with a frown. "It's past nine, so I'm surprised that they aren't home, but it is Friday night. Date night, maybe?"

I shook my head. "No, not really. Maybe we could try my brother? We can get his number from the local directory."

"Better not to get anyone else involved if we can help it," Jack said, crossing his arms. "Do they have any favorite restaurants they'd be at, anything like that?"

"There is one thing," I said slowly. "Where's the tablet?" Without waiting for an answer, I jumped up and jogged into the kitchen where I'd left it. I laid the tablet on the coffee table so Jack wouldn't see how bad my hands were shaking as I typed in the group's website, then navigated to the "Events" tab to find my worst fears confirmed. "Shit!" I jumped to my feet to stomp around the living room.

"What?" Jack leaned over the tablet and read the page out loud. "May Crown Tournament." He looked up at me with an amused smile. "Your parents are role-players?"

"Kinda. My mom loves period costuming and sewing, and the group is a great excuse for her to sew new outfits for the whole family." Feeling a little better for the stomping, I knelt on the other side of the coffee table to reach the tablet. I scrolled down the page and pointed to a line in the schedule. "That's why they aren't home and aren't answering their phones."

"Bardic circle," Jack read, then glanced back up at me, a small smile tugging at his lips. "I don't know that dressing up and singing merit that deep of a scowl."

"It's not the singing, it's the damn dressing up." I pushed up from the coffee table and glared down at the tablet. "Growing up, she was always dragging me to those things. After five boys, I was her only 'girl'," I made air quotes around the word, "and she was so excited to make dresses for me. She treated me like her doll. Frilly lace and corsets, and god, I hated it so much." I felt like punching something just talking about it. Stomping across the room helped only so much. "We were always fighting about it." I scowled harder and crossed my arms.

"Well, no dressing up this time," Jack said in an understanding voice.

"So what does this circle have to do with not answering their phones?"

"It's really discouraged to answer a cellphone at these events, especially at the bardic circles."

"So we leave them a message telling them they are in danger, and to go to the police." Jack bent over the tablet again. "This says quiet hours start at ten, so they'll get the message when they get home for the night.

I groaned. "Knowing how seriously my mom takes these things, they left their phones at home. Besides, the police are a bad idea. Lady Ann has cops on her payroll. Remember those cops who showed up at my apartment?"

Jack nodded.

"Remember I told you I went to talk to one of them? They work for her." I moved around to sit back down next to Jack and covered my face with my hands. "How are we going to get a message to them now?"

"You mentioned five brothers? Do they all live in town?"

I leaned forward to rest my elbows on my knees. "No, just my brother Michael, two years older than me. He works at Dad's garage. All my other brothers moved away. They're scattered all over the country. Why?"

"Just trying to figure out who else she might go after next." Jack sighed. "Alright, let's give your brother Michael a call, since he'd be the next logical choice for her to go after anyway."

"Thank you." I raised my head and gave Jack a grateful smile.

I looked up Michael's number through my email account, since my cellphone was long gone, and read the number off to Jack. I reached for the phone, but Jack shook his head, switching hands to hold the phone on the side away from me. "No, too dangerous. In case he's already involved, let me do the—"

Michael must have answered, because Jack cut himself off abruptly.

"Hello, Michael? This is Detective Jack Petty." There was a pause.

I raised my eyebrows at this lie. Jack saw and waved me off with a smile. "No, the reason I'm calling is about your brother, Everett."

"What!" I blurted out. Jack's free hand swung up and clamped over my mouth before I could say anything else.

"Sorry about that. Yes, no, your brother is fine. He's in police custody right now—"

Jack glanced at me. I lifted a hand to make a zipping motion across my lips. Jack nodded and let go.

"So you haven't seen the news?" Jack asked, and then paused again. I was dying of curiosity about what my brother was saying on the other end of the line. Why didn't vampires get enhanced hearing like the movies? I leaned closer, trying to hear, but Jack pushed me away.

"I don't have time to go over the details of your brother's case with you at this time. I'm calling you about another urgent matter. We have reason to suspect that you and your parents' lives are in danger. However, we've been unable to reach your parents. Where are you right now?"

Jack glanced at me and frowned. "Well, that is good news. Please stay where you are for now. You should be safe in Miami. We have reason to believe the threat is local to Portland."

Another pause, and I fidgeted nervously. My stomach sank at the mention of Miami. Although I was happy that Michael was out of town, which should mean he would be out of Lady Ann's reach, it meant that he couldn't go by and warn our parents. I hoped this was for the gay cruise he'd mentioned last time we'd talked. He deserved to be able to cut loose away from our ultra-conservative parents.

"Yes, do you have any other way to reach them?" Jack paused again. "Hood River County Fairgrounds, got it. We'll send a few officers by there to check on them. Thank you for the information."

Jack hung up and lowered the phone, then gave me a sympathetic look. "I take it you overheard? Michael confirmed your hunch about where your parents are. He said the only way to reach them is going to be going by in person. The good news is that he's on vacation in Miami, so he'll be safe."

"So, who can we call?" I stared back at Jack. "And who's Jack Petty? I thought from that memory I saw that your last name is Prashad."

"It was Prashad. Since I went into the supernatural's version of wit-sec for outed supernaturals, it's been Jack Smith."

I made a face and Jack laughed.

"I know, believe me, but I didn't get a choice. They insisted on nice and generic. I'm just glad they let me keep my first name. Anyway, I'm not going to give out my real name, am I?"

"I guess not, but you didn't answer my first question."

"I didn't answer because we aren't going to do anything else. We've pushed our luck as it is." Jack held up a hand to forestall my protests. "We can't get anyone else involved, and we have no way to warn them by phone."

"It's only an hour's drive up there," I pleaded. "We go up there, warn them, come back. No one even has to know we left."

"I'd know." Jack looked uncomfortable. "It's just too dangerous. You know she's going to have people watching them. Besides, we both know that a warning probably won't make any difference. If she wants them dead, there's really nothing we can do to stop it."

"So why help me try to call them?" I clasped my hands together and made a pleading look.

"Everett, I was helping you mostly for your piece of mind. You're just going to have to accept the fact that you won't get to make up with them."

"If we disguise ourselves, they won't know who we are. Besides, they'll be looking for one person, not two."

Jack shook his head. "No."

"I can use my speed to get in and out. Lady Ann's thugs will be human. They'll never even see me." I lifted my hand, palm towards Jack, and put the other one over my heart. "Scout's honor."

"Alright, let's play this game." Jack shifted to face me. He started ticking points off on his finger. "If you manage to speed or sneak past the guards— who are by the way, probably well-trained mercenaries or ex-military—and then if you manage to find your parents' tent in a dark field filled with near identical tents, how do you convince them of the danger?"

I frowned and stayed silent for a moment while Jack looked at me expectantly. "Well, Michael seemed to take you seriously," I said finally.

Jack shook his head. "He thought I was a cop. These are your parents who from the sound of things, haven't listened to you very well in the past." Jack waved a hand. "Okay, let's skip that and pretend they do listen. How do you get them to safety, back out past Lady Ann's guards? Without," Jack fixed me with a glare, "revealing you are a vampire. Top secret, remember?"

"I guess I didn't think that far ahead," I admitted. "Forewarned is forearmed. Once they know about the threat, they should be okay, right?"

"You're the youngest of six, was it?"

I nodded, not seeing where Jack was going. "Yeah, so?"

"How old are your parents, Everett?"

"They're both almost sixty, but my dad's a mechanic, and keeps in shape. My mom's really active too. She walks a mile every morning."

"You think they're a match for trained fighters?"

I threw up my hands in frustration. "You keep mentioning mercenaries, but we don't know that. She's a mobster, she doesn't have an army. For all we know, she might not even have anyone there." Saying that gave me another idea. "Wait, maybe she doesn't. What if we just go up there and check it out, take out anyone who looks like a threat? Then I wouldn't even have to talk to my parents."

"The ones who took me were professionals, but—" Jack closed his eyes and squeezed the bridge of his nose with one hand. "Everett... You seem to be missing my point." He opened his eyes and took my hands in his. "You can't save them. We've done all we can. Now we just sit tight."

"But—" I tried to pull away, but Jack squeezed my hands and gave me a sad look.

"Everett, I know you don't want to lose them, but I want you to understand something." He leaned closer and rested his forehead against mine. "I don't want to lose you, either."

I started shaking, and Jack put his arms around me and pulled me close.

"What if—"

"No, Everett. We can't risk it."

I swallowed. "I just want to talk to them. I sneak in, say my piece, and then get out."

"Damn you, Everett. We agreed it's a risk." Jack tightened his arms around me and began massaging my shoulders.

"I know." I leaned back into Jack. "I know it's dangerous, but I just want to see my parents one last time. Have a chance to make peace with them."

Jack sighed heavily. "I understand. I want to help you, but it doesn't matter without a car to get up there."

"You don't have a car?" I sat back to regard him. "How did you get to the grocery store then?"

Jack laughed. "I walked. My car got mysteriously filled with bullet holes, remember?"

I stuck my tongue out at him. "If we get a car, you'll agree to help?"

"You're so stubborn, and you look before you leap." Jack sighed. "I love it about you. I even like how bad you are at lying, although we are going to have to work on changing that if you're going to keep your vampire nature a secret. But yes, I can understand. If I could go back, I'd want one last chance to see my parents."

I chewed my lip. "So what now?"

"Let's get a car." Jack pulled out a phone and started scrolling through the contacts. "Too late to rent one, and everyone you know is out, obviously. Problem is, I'm still pretty new to town, and most of the people I know are connected to the office. We don't want Stacy getting wind of this, so that narrows the list considerably."

"The only person I've talked to that isn't part of the offices is Emily. Or would she still be at the offices?" I said slowly.

"Not a bad idea. She fell asleep at the wheel and her car hit the freeway dividers. Not serious and the airbags went off, so she wasn't hurt, just startled enough to trigger her transformation. Meant there weren't any witnesses, so she could just go back to her life."

"Wait, if she crashed, her car won't be drivable."

"I talked more with her after you went to bed. She has to drive a lot for work. I bet she already has a new one by now, or at least a rental we could borrow."

Jack scrolled to her name and lifted the phone to his ear.

"Hello, Emily. This is Jack. From PCA. Yes. How are you doing?"

Jack nodded along to her words, smiling. "Good, good. Listen, I have a favor to ask. My car broke down, and Everett and I need to run up to Mount Hood tonight." There was another pause. "Yes, exactly. That would be great. It's near Lloyd center. I'll text you the address. Right then, see you soon." He hung up and turned to me, smiling. "She is happy to lend us a car.

She'll be picking us up in fifteen."

EMILY HONKED WHEN SHE arrived, pulling up in a brand-new white sedan with a temporary plate taped in the rear window. Jack and I went out to meet her. She smiled warmly at Jack as she got out of the driver's side, but her smile faded when she nodded her head to me.

Emily looked much better today. Her hair was done up, and she wore understated makeup and a professional suit. I was surprised, given how late it was, that she looked like she'd come straight from an office.

"Just drop me at the train station by the mall," Emily said, leaning forward to talk to Jack over his shoulder as he adjusted her seat and mirrors to fit his taller frame. "I sent you my address, so bring the car back to me there in the morning when you get back." She sat back again, giving me a side-eyed look.

"Thanks, Emily. We really appreciate it," Jack said, starting the car up.

"I mean, I don't mind helping you out, but why is he going with you?" Emily wrinkled her nose. "Zoe told me he's a vampire. Is that why he stunk when I was a fox?"

"That's right," Jack said, backing into the street. "Our noses in our animal forms can smell that vampires are dead, and instinctively we dislike it. Part of why vampires and shapeshifters were at odds for so long."

Emily's face scrunched further. "It's not going to linger in my car, is it?"

"Afraid so." Jack glanced at Emily in the rearview mirror.

"Hey!" I protested, but Jack kept talking.

"Sorry. But the good news is that you'll only smell it when you're in your animal form. Plus, it'll be good for you to get used to it. As you can see, vampires get a little testy when you imply that they stink." Jack's eyes canted over to me. "Everett, not your fault. Just stating facts."

"Fine." Emily crossed her arms.

"What is it you do for work, Emily?" I asked, trying to reduce the tension that was growing in the car.

"I saw you on the news." Emily glared at me.

I slid down in my seat. "I'm innocent," I mumbled.

"That news report has to do with why I'm taking him to Mount Hood," Jack said, reaching over with one hand to rub my leg for a moment, before putting it back on the wheel. "But the details are up to him to reveal."

I shook my head. "Maybe another time," I mumbled.

Jack took pity on me. "Emily is a real estate agent."

"That's why I'm out so late. A lot of people only want to see houses after they get off work, so I'm often working in the evenings."

Jack turned down the street near the mall and pulled over to the side of the road. "Here you go, Emily. Thanks again for letting us borrow your car."

Emily opened her door, but lingered inside. "I have a showing at eleven tomorrow."

"I'll have it back first thing in the morning, promise," Jack said.

Emily nodded. "I'll hold you to that. And Everett?" She looked directly at me for the first time. "Good luck on getting your name cleared."

"Thanks."

She got out and walked away, while Jack put the car back into gear and headed for the freeway.

CHAPTER 18

THE REN FAIRE

WITH JACK DRIVING LIKE a bat out of hell and light traffic on I-84 eastbound, we managed to make it up to Hood River in less than an hour, rolling into town just before 10:00 pm. I directed him to the fairgrounds from memory. I'd been dragged there enough times over the first eighteen years of my life for various Renaissance Fairs and SCA Events that I could probably have found my way there blindfolded.

Quiet hours were beginning as we arrived, but many people were still out and about, mostly gathered around the bonfires scattered around one edge of the fairground. Jack parked at the end of the line of cars and turned off the engine but grabbed my arm before I could open the door.

"Ground rules. First, no revealing your nature or anything about the supernatural. Second, this is just for you to make up with them. Third, we go straight back to the safe house after." Jack gave me a hard look, narrowing his eyes at me. "Got it?"

"Got it. But what will you do while I find them? Are you just going to wait in the car?" I asked.

"And leave you on your own?" Jack gave me a bemused look. "No. I'm going with you."

"She knows you too. Won't that give us a greater chance of being recognized?"

"Yes, but I won't feel safe with you by yourself. I can protect myself if need be." Jack glanced around outside, craning around to check the back too. A few people were smoking in front of a car a row down, but they had their backs turned to us and seemed to be focused on their own conversation. "Let's go. Keep your head down and act casual."

We both got out of the car and walked toward the fires. It was dark out here in the country, and the moon was down to just a sliver tonight so there was hardly any moonlight, but to my surprise I could still see almost perfectly. Jack stumbled on the uneven ground, so I took his arm.

"I can see. Just hold on to me."

Jack gave me a grateful smile and wrapped his arm in mine and took my hand. I was glad he couldn't see me in the dark, since I was sure I had a goofy smile on my face.

My parents had owned the same tent for years, and I'd recognize it if I saw it. However, first I steered Jack toward the bonfires. Despite the lateness of the hour, that was where we were most likely to find them. My mother loved to socialize, and was always one of the last to turn in.

We neared the fire with the biggest group of people around it. With my new vampire vision, the light of the fire actually made it harder for me to see; pure darkness seemed to be better for my new eyes. Then someone stepped aside, revealing two profiles. I stopped abruptly, recognizing my mother and father. My mother was shorter even than my barely five-foot height, and combined with the big, poufy dress meant it couldn't be anyone else. My much-taller father stood next to her, wearing what I had always joked was his pirate coat, which was buttoned tight against the night's chill.

Jack leaned down and whispered in my ear, "What's wrong?"

"I spotted my parents." I jerked his head toward them. "We can wait here and tail them back to their tent."

"No, we need to get this over with. I recognize that tall muscular guy over there. He was one of the men who abducted me." Jack's eyes flicked in the man's direction, and I turned to follow his gaze. "No, don't look."

I jerked my head back, trying to glance over with just my eyes as Jack pulled me along again in the direction of my parents. Jack was right, I was terrible at this. I hadn't even spotted the man, although now that Jack had pointed him out, it was obvious he didn't belong here. He looked very uncomfortable in his obviously brand-new, store-bought doublet. A strange bulge in the shirt's side could only be a gun.

We were almost to my parents when a man and a woman stepped out of the crowd, stopping directly in our path. I moved to go around them, but the woman's arm shot out, blocking the way.

"Who are you?" she hissed, glaring at me. "And why do I feel so drawn to you?"

I stared back at her. I could almost feel the animosity coming off her and the man in waves. "Do I know you?" I craned my neck to see around her and make sure I didn't lose track of my parents.

"No, that's the problem." The woman glared at me and put her hands on her hips. "You should have sent in notice if you wanted to attend an event outside your home area." The man with her was nodding along to her words.

"What are you talking about?" I said, glancing over at Jack to see if he was as confused as I was.

Jack looked like he'd bit a sour lemon. He leaned toward me. "They're vampires, Ev."

Oh, right. I could see it now. Both of them were pale under their makeup, and the firelight reflected off their eyes with an odd sheen.

"I'm sorry, I'm new. I didn't know the rules." I pushed her arm out of the way. "But I'm in a hurry, and we're not staying."

The man with her, dressed as a Victorian nobleman, was suddenly standing in front of me. He grabbed my arm, his grip like iron.

"Stop," Jack said softly. "It's fine, he's with me. I'm Jack Smith, from the PCA." When both vampires looked at him blankly, he continued. "I work for Stacy Cord."

Both lit with comprehension, but the woman frowned.

"Why's he being escorted in our territory by a mangy mutt instead of a vampire?" she sneered.

Jack let out a growl, his eyes flashing dangerously. He gritted his teeth, and I could see the effort it was taking him not to respond to the insult. "They're busy tracking down that rogue vampire. Like you should be doing."

The man had the grace to look guilty, although the woman merely tossed her head, making her blond curls bounce, and pouted. "Like I'd miss the event of the season. I'd have to wait months for the next chance to show off my new outfit to people who can appreciate it." She posed a little and I, who'd grown up with a seamstress mother who was a period perfectionist, could see why she was so proud of it. It was deep red with a low-cut corset, a big bustle with at least a dozen layers of petticoats, and wide-sleeves. Wait, I recognized that hand-stitching on the sleeves.

"It is fabulous. You look amazing. I can see why you want to show it off." I smiled at her. "It fits you perfectly. Your seamstress did an excellent job."

The woman's chest swelled and she batted her eyelashes at me before smirking at Jack. "I'm glad to see someone can appreciate quality."

"I'd love to get one for myself." I glanced at the man still holding my arm. "That's why I'm here, actually. To see Mrs. Boesch. I just want to talk to her and then we'll be going."

"Not going to stay for Cloved Fruit?" the man said in a thick British accent, finally letting go of my arm. "It's the highlight of the evening, isn't it, Clarissa?"

Jack looked down at me in confusion. Cloved Fruit was a sexy drinking game popular at Ren Fairs. I could see why vampires enjoyed it, but there wasn't time to explain all that to Jack now. I shook my head, mouthing "later" at him, and then said, "No, maybe next time."

"More for us then, Reggie." Clarissa took Reggie's arm again, giving me a critical once-over. "If I may give you a bit of advice: ask for an outfit that'll go with heeled boots. A bit of height will help you win over the ladies better."

Jack let out a guffaw that he badly covered up with a cough. "After you then, ma'am."

Clarissa gave Jack a dirty look, but escorted us over to my mother and father, who were talking to a man I didn't recognize. I overheard her say, "I haven't seen her," before Clarissa walked right between her and the man she was speaking to, cutting her off mid-sentence.

"Rose, good evening. This young gentleman," Clarissa gestured to me, "was just admiring the new outfits you made for Reggie and me. He just had to meet the designer to get one of his own."

My mother had a smile on her face as she looked at Clarissa, but as soon as I stepped out of Jack's shadow and into the firelight, the smile slid off her face and she wrinkled her nose as if she'd just stepped in something disgusting.

"I won't speak to that thing," she sniffed, "until my daughter returns."

Even Clarissa looked taken aback at vehemence in my mother's tone. Well, this reunion was off to a great start. At least my father was looking at me. I decided to start there. I turned to him with a pleading look. Sometimes my father could talk sense into my mother. I felt, more than saw, Jack move to stand next to me.

"Dad, I wanted to see you to—"

"You heard your mother," my father said mildly. He was almost expressionless. My mother lifted her nose in the air and turned her back to me, picking up her skirt in both hands and walking away. My father gave me a small frown as he looked me over, taking in my scraggly five-o-clock shadow that had taken me two weeks of cultivating to grow, and my chest, flattened by my makeshift binder. "Come back to us dressed as a proper young lady again, then we can talk." He turned and hurried after my mother.

All the air left my lungs, and I felt like I was going to puke. Then I wondered if vampires could throw up.

"Dad? You idiot!" Clarissa leaned down to hiss at me. She was angry because she thought I'd faked my death before being turned, as was common practice. She didn't know that wasn't the case with me. "And you, how could you be a part of this?" she demanded, whirling on Jack.

"I agree, he is an idiot," a man said from behind me, followed by the click of a gun being cocked. "All of you, put your hands in the air."

My eyes went wide and I glanced at Jack, who was glaring at me in an I-told-you-so way as he raised his hands above his head. I did the same, as did Clarissa and Reggie, who both looked slightly confused.

"Turn around, slowly."

All four of us did so to find the man my parents had been speaking with holding us all at gunpoint. He waved the tip of the gun first at Clarissa and Reggie, and then at Jack. "You three, get out of here. I only need this one." He settled the barrel back to point directly at my face.

Clarissa nodded, gathering her bustle in one hand and grabbing Reggie's hand in the other. She frowned at me for a moment, but then shrugged, and she and Reggie almost ran away.

The man watched them go for a second, then glanced at Jack. "You too."

"I won't leave him." Jack stepped between me and the gun. "Run, Ev." The man's gun barked, and Jack grunted in pain and staggered back.

"Not without you!" I grabbed Jack around the waist, letting myself sink into the near-fugue state that let me move so fast. I tossed Jack over my shoulder and dashed in the direction of the car. It was a bit awkward, since Jack was nearly a foot taller than me. Jack seemed heavier than he should have, especially with the way I'd thrown around that cop the other night, but he wasn't unmanageably heavy, although it did slow me down.

Something warm ran down my back, and I smelled Jack's blood. I couldn't stop my fangs from descending. The gun cracked again. Pain blossomed up my arm, and I nearly dropped Jack. Something soft hit the back of my head and exploded, showering me with something wet. Had he thrown a water balloon at me?

People around the camp began screaming and running away from the shots. Lights began to go on all around the camp, heads popping out of tents as I wove around through the campground toward the car. I hoped the darkness made it so that no one noticed that I was running faster than the rest of the crowd.

I was going so fast that I almost crashed into the car, sliding on the loose gravel for a moment before falling against the trunk.

My right arm refused to move, forcing me to clumsily dump Jack sideways onto the ground. Jack moaned as he hit, and the strong smell of blood nearly made me swoon. Jack landed on his side. The front of his shirt had a neat hole in the front, and a trail of blood tracked up his chest.

I cursed and knelt down, applying pressure to the wound with my working hand. Jack's eyes were fluttering and he was unresponsive.

"Don't die, Jack," I babbled, pressing on the bloody hole in Jack's chest with my good hand.

Then Jack's chest sunk in, and fur sprouted up from his face as his nose elongated. A moment later, a jackal lay there in Jack's bloody clothes. It began thrashing in slow motion around in them, trying to get loose.

The screams began to get closer, and I looked up to see three men with guns moving through the crowd in our direction. They looked to be moving with exaggerated slowness, but it wouldn't take them long to get into range, and they were already raising their guns. One had another water balloon out, and had his arm cocked back to throw it. Why water balloons? I didn't have time to dwell on it now.

"Shit, keys." I fumbled at Jack's pants with my one working hand, trying to ignore the way the jackal was glaring at me. I finally got ahold of the keyring and tugged it free. I unlocked the car, and turned to get the jackal.

I grabbed Jack's bloody clothes as a bundle, slow-motion jackal and all, and tossed the whole thing into the passenger seat without looking. Jack's yelp of surprise seemed to go on forever while I climbed inside and got the car started. I was starting to get so thirsty, but if I slowed down, the men would get to the car before I'd be able to get us out of here.

A gun cracked, and the car jumped as the bullet impacted somewhere I couldn't see.

My right arm still refused to move, so I had to awkwardly twist my left hand around in order to get the key in the ignition, frantically glancing at the slowly approaching men as I struggled to reach around the steering wheel. At least the car started right up.

As soon as I got it into reverse, I floored it, sending us careening backward into the road. I was starting to get some sensation back, but it still took me a moment to pop the shifter into drive with my partially numb right hand. I let my speed fall away as I hit the gas and roared away. Bullets whizzed after us as the three men chased us down the road, firing at the retreating car until they were out of view.

Jack jumped up into the passenger seat and sat down, having finally wiggled his way free of his clothing. His hackles were up and his lips were pulled back from his muzzle as if he were growling, although I couldn't hear anything.

"I know, I know. You told me so," I said to the jackal, slurring around the unfamiliar feel of my fangs, which refused to retract.

CHAPTER 19

TIGER, BURNING BRIGHT

JACK MADE ME DRIVE back the long way, around south of Mount Hood, since he rightly pointed out that Lady Ann would most likely be having I-84 watched, which added another hour onto the drive. Jack napped on the passenger's seat as a jackal while I drove. After I determined he wasn't hurt, I let him sleep. Shapeshifting healed most injuries, but was tiring.

My arm ached. It was odd. When I'd been shot through the heart, it'd hurt, sure, but not like this. A tingling pain was spreading down my arm and back. The pain became so bad I had to pull over to the side of the narrow highway to lay back against the seat. Closing my eyes, I gritted my teeth, waiting for the worst of it to pass.

Sometime later I felt a warm nose press against my face.

"Everett?" Jack said.

I opened my eyes to find Jack's jackal muzzle inches from my face. I shied to the side in alarm.

"Are you okay? You look very pale—well, more than normal," Jack clarified.

"Shoulder." I had to pause as a wave of pain wracked me. "Hurts. Shot."

"Shot? You should have healed." Jack's long ears went back and he backed up, claws clicking on the center console. "Sit forward. Let me see."

I was only too happy to slump forward over the steering wheel so that

Jack could inspect my bullet wound. I felt whiskers on my back as Jack ripped my shirt open with his teeth.

"Water balloon too," I gasped.

"It's black around the wound. Silver, most likely," Jack said. "And it's a myth about holy water, if that was what was in those balloons."

"Silver?" I slurred. "You. Shot. Too." It took me several breaths to get the whole sentence out.

"Yeah, but the myth about silver and were creatures is just that: a myth. Silver doesn't hurt shapeshifters any more than a regular bullet." Jack's breath was warm on my back. "But not for vampires. Only saving grace is it looks like a through and through. We just have to get you some blood and wait for the trace amounts of silver to make their way out of your system."

There was a shuffling sound, and I only half listened to what Jack was doing. A door slammed and then Jack grabbed my head from behind, wrapping my whole face with a cloth. Strong arms pulled me out of the driver's seat. I could feel his warmth and his pulse where he held me. So thirsty. I salivated. My fangs were already down.

I clawed and snapped, trying to bite the meal holding me, but the cloth around my face was in the way. After a moment my brain processed that I needed to move the cloth before I could eat, but my working hand was trapped between my body and the food holding me. Then suddenly I was falling, and landed on my bad arm. My scream was louder even than the sound of the trunk slamming shut over me.

"I'm sorry, Everett." A door slammed and the car started up again.

My left arm was free. I tore the covering from my face to find myself lying on my side in a pitch-dark trunk. I could still see the outlines of things around me, like at the fairgrounds. The warm food was close, so close, but as much as I tried, I couldn't claw through the metal barrier between me and it. Dimly I was aware of the car moving, bouncing along, but my overriding need for the warmth of blood on my tongue drowned out almost everything else.

A WHILE LATER THE trunk popped open, letting in a sliver of light. I thrashed, kicking, trying to open it more, while snapping my teeth at the warm thing on the other side. Two red bottles that smelled like blood were pushed through the opening, then the trunk was slammed closed again. I attacked the nearest bottle, greedily gulping down the contents.

By the time I finished the second one, I'd come back to myself a bit. I lay there, panting as I remembered trying to bite Jack. I hadn't even processed at that time that it had been Jack. At the time, all I'd known was that he was food.

"Awfully quiet in there. Are you finally calm?" Jack asked from outside.

"I think so," I said, curling on my side away from the opening and hugging my knees to my chest as I stared at the ruined trunk. In my frenzy I'd clawed through the cloth covering on the back inside of the trunk, and I could see fingernail scratches in the metal of the interior. Between this, the blood, and the bullet holes, Emily was going to be pissed.

"Think so or know so?" Jack asked.

I stared at the devastation around me. "I didn't even know it was you," I said, biting back a sob. "I'm sorry."

The lock clicked and the trunk swung open. "You were thirsty and in pain. It happens. Come on. We need to get you inside before dawn."

I let Jack help me out. Jack wore his blood-stained pants, but no shirt. Yet even the sight of shirtless Jack couldn't overcome the wave of misery that swept over me. I turned my head away, unable to look at him as he escorted me to the basement door.

"You still look awful. I'll send down another bottle. Drink it before you lie down, okay?" Jack said in a motherly voice.

I just went down the stairs without responding.

"Do you want to talk about what happened with your parents?" Jack took two steps down after me. I could hear the hurt in his voice.

"No." I didn't look back.

Jack sighed. I heard him walk back up the stairs and shut the door behind him. I winced when the lock clicked shut, bursting into tears as I realized that Jack was afraid of me. I made it to the bottom of the steps before collapsing down into a heap on the floor. I curled up into a fetal position, feeling numb. Wrung out. Empty. Not only did my parents still hate me, now Jack did too.

The upstairs door creaked open sometime later, and then hesitant footsteps thumped down the steps. "Everett," Jack said tenderly. There was the sound of him setting something down.

"Go away," I gasped between sobs. "I don't want to eat you."

Jack sat down on the bottom step and pulled me up against his chest, wrapping his arms around my crossed arms. "You aren't going to eat me."

"Yes I am. That's why you're afraid of me now." I half-heartedly pushed at Jack's arms, but I didn't really want him to stop. I felt safe. Protected.

"Look, if I were afraid of you, would I be down here right now?" He rested his chin on my shoulder and his arms tightened around me.

"But you locked me in the trunk. And I did try to eat you earlier." I sniffed.

"I respect your power as a vampire. There's a difference. You don't try to reason with a hungry tiger, after all." Jack's voice was light, but I could feel the tension under the words. I'd scared Jack, even if he wasn't admitting it now.

"Did you just compare me to a tiger?" I let out a giggle between sobs, despite myself.

"Yes, I did." Jack rubbed his beard against my cheek. "My fierce tiger. I don't blame you. You were in pain and starving. I'm not going to blame you for not being rational. You pushed yourself far too hard, using your speed for that long to save me. Besides, would you rather I have let you eat me?"

I shuddered as I pictured coming back to myself to find Jack dead by my hand. "No. No, I wouldn't have."

"So would you like to talk about it?" Jack said softly.

I swallowed. "Not really. It was terrifying. I didn't even realize it was you. I just sensed food nearby and wanted it."

Jack sighed. "Not what I was talking about, Everett. Your parents—"

"No." Now I did push out of Jack's embrace, jumping to my feet and walking away. I stopped a few feet away with my head bowed. "I was a fool for expecting anything else from them. It's my fault."

"That's not true." Jack got up and followed me. "But I respect your wish to not talk about it now." He walked around me and thrust a red bottle into my hands. "Here, I brought this down for you. You lost a lot of blood between the bullet and using your powers. It'll help flush the silver out of your system too."

I sighed and nodded, making a face before starting to chug the contents. I hadn't felt thirsty, but I did start to feel better, perkier, than I had been before drinking it.

Jack's mouth quirked up in a one-sided smile at my expression. "Stacy hates those things too." He held up his other hand so I could see the first aid kit he held. "When you're done, sit down on the couch so I can bandage you up."

I threw the empty squeeze bottle in the trash and sat on the couch.

"Shirt off," Jack said, sitting next to me.

I blushed. "Um, can I leave my binder on?"

Jack frowned. "Shirt off first, then we'll see."

I sighed but stripped my shirt off, crying out in pain when I lifted my right arm up. "Shit, that hurts still." I craned my head to see the bullet wound in my shoulder. Dark blood leaked slowly from a jagged hole in my collarbone, and ran down my back and over my binder. Black lines radiated out from the hole along my skin, going almost a palm's length down my upper arm and chest.

Jack gently put his hand on my back, turning me so that my back was to him. "You can leave the binder on; the wound is high enough it missed it. Now sit still. I'm not sure if this will hurt; I don't know a lot about vampires. I'm going to clean it with antiseptic wipes."

"Okay," I said, clenching my fists and gritting my teeth to prepare. Something wet hit my shoulder. "Nothing yet."

"Good." Jack began gently rubbing the cloth along my shoulder. "I'm going to touch the wound next. It looks better than it did earlier, so you are healing."

"This is better?" I asked, but then Jack's ministrations reached the hole in my back and I had to bite back a scream. It felt like someone was poking a stick through my back.

"You're doing great."

Jack finally finished, and I gasped in relief when he lifted off the antiseptic cloth so he could slap a bandage over the wound. "Now the front."

"Great," I muttered, but turned around to face Jack, who turned a bit red.

"Too far." He gently pressed a hand on my uninjured shoulder to turn me so that he could reach my wounded shoulder better. He cleaned it quickly and efficiently, although it hurt like the devil again, and I had to close my eyes and grit my teeth against the pain.

What felt like a thousand years later, Jack put a square bandage over the front hole. "There. Done. You did great."

Jack glanced at the clock on the wall. "We need to get you to bed. C'mon." He helped me stand then took me to bed, tucking me in.

He paused in the doorway on his way out and turned to look back at me lying in bed, staring at the ceiling. "Are you sure you're alright, Everett?"

"Not really?" I rolled over onto my good shoulder, putting my back to Jack. "Why does it hurt so much, even though it's nothing worse than they said to me last year?"

The bed settled as Jack lay down behind me. He spooned me from behind, being careful when he put his arm around my waist not to bump my hurt shoulder. I relaxed into his embrace. It felt intimate, despite the blankets separating us. We lay there in silence for a long moment.

"Because they're your parents. We're always told that they'll love you no matter what. It hurts a lot when that love turns out to be conditional," Jack said finally.

"Did your parents... How did they react to you coming out?" I asked softly. I tried to tug my arm free of the covers, wanting to clasp Jack's hand, but my shoulder screamed in agony when I tried to move.

"Not well at first, but they came around. Although my mom never stopped harping on me about how my decision denied her grand babies. I was an only child, but still." Jack blew out a breath. "As if I chose to be gay. Anyway, nothing like what you're going through. I wish I knew what to say to you, other than to tell you it's not your fault."

"Thanks," I said sleepily. Jack's words helped, even if it was the comfort of knowing not all parents rejected their queer children.

I rolled over to lie on my back, turning my head to look at Jack, who smiled down at me tenderly. "About that date…" I let my words trail off. Jack probably wasn't in the mood, but I didn't want him to leave.

Jack gave me a sad smile. "I hope you don't consider tonight our first date."

"No." I glanced away, blushing. "Not so far, but maybe it can start now?"

Jack glanced at the clock on the wall. "Only twenty minutes till sunrise, not much of a tonight left. And you're injured."

I gave him a shy smile. "I'm feeling a lot better."

"Fine, but we'll take it slow." Jack propped himself up on an elbow and leaned over to kiss me. His mustache and beard tickled my face pleasantly.

I tugged my left arm out of the covers and reached up to caress Jack's face. His tongue probed my lips, and I parted them to let Jack explore further. I shifted right, and winced when that jostled my hurt arm. Jack immediately pulled back and looked down at me with concern.

"I'm fine," I said, reaching up to grab Jack's hair and pulling his head back down to resume our kissing. Jack smiled and let me.

The kisses got hotter and deeper, then Jack pulled away.

"These covers are in the way," he muttered. He stripped the covers down and tossed them off the edge of the bed. I blushed as my binder was exposed, even though Jack had already seen it earlier. Jack knelt on the bed and looked me over with a smile. "You're so cute," he whispered.

"How 'bout you lose that shirt?" I said back. "I'm feeling a little underdressed compared to you."

"Deal." Jack put his hands behind his head and tugged his shirt off, dropping it off the bed. He crawled over and straddled my hips. He put a finger on the edge of the compression back brace that I was using as a makeshift binder and ran it along the lower edge, giving me a questioning look.

"I want to leave it on," I whispered, putting my right hand over Jack's. The movement twinged my shoulder a little, but it wasn't unbearable.

Jack smiled at me and set a hand on the bed on either side of my chest and leaned forward over me. "That's fine. I could tell me touching it last night bothered you too. Is that why you changed your mind about sex yesterday? You'd been all raring to go before that."

I nodded and bit my lip, waiting for Jack to stand up and reject me because of it. It was what had happened with every guy I'd met at the gay bars after I started passing more often than not. When they'd found boobs where they expected none, rejection quickly followed. Instead Jack just gave me a tender smile, then bent down to kiss me. His hips ground against mine, his erection hard enough I could feel it pressing against me, even through both our jeans. My own underwear was damp with need, and I shifted my hips to grind Jack's erection against my crotch.

I lifted my good arm and ran my hand along Jack's bare chest, ruffling Jack's chest hair, until I found one of his nipples. I ran a finger around the edge of it. Jack broke apart our kiss with a gasp and sat up to fumble with the front of his jeans. Without getting up off me, he stripped them off one leg at a time to reveal Pokémon-branded boxer briefs that barely contained his erect cock. While he did that I tried to unbutton my own pants, but it was too difficult with just one hand.

"Need a little help with that?" Jack smirked as he kicked off the last leg of his jeans.

"Please." I lifted my hand and let Jack unbutton and unzip my pants. I bent my knees and set my feet so I could lift my hips, allowing Jack to yank them off. He pulled my underwear off at the same time, leaving me naked on the bed except for my binder. I flushed and grabbed the waistband of Jack's briefs. "Hey, no fair."

"True." Jack pulled them off and tossed them away, then straddled my hips again. His throbbing, hard cock rested on my stomach and I grabbed it, gently running my hand up and down it.

Jack groaned, rocking his hips against mine. "Grip it harder." I tightened my grip and Jack moaned. "Yes, much better."

"It looks different than the ones I've seen in porn," I said without thinking. I immediately blushed and added, "It's nice. I like it."

Thankfully Jack just laughed. "I haven't been circumcised. That's the difference. See that flap of skin near the head that's moving with your hand?" I nodded. "That's the foreskin."

"I'm glad you aren't offended. It's my first time with a guy, after all." I kept stroking Jack's erection, enjoying the way it felt in my hand and the way Jack moved against my hips. Wetness slicked the inside of my thighs as Jack's butt rubbed my legs and his hips rocked against mine.

"It'll be a first for both of us," Jack said, leaning back over me to rest his weight on his hands. His cock got pinned between his bare chest and my stomach, forcing me to let go of it. Jack kissed me lightly on the lips. "I'll answer any of your questions as long as you answer mine."

"Deal," I agreed, running both my hands down Jack's sides now. My shoulder ached but I ignored it, having too much fun to want to stop. I could only reach as far as Jack's waist, and wished I were taller so that I could cup Jack's ass in my hand.

"What would you like me to do?" Jack asked, giving the bandage on my shoulder a significant glance. "Within reason."

I bit my lip. "I want you inside me."

Jack nodded, and leaned over to give me another deep kiss with tongue. His cock pulsed against me. This close the smell of Jack's blood was overwhelming, and without meaning to my fangs descended, pricking Jack's lip as he kissed me.

"Oww." Jack pulled away and touched his lip, fingers coming away red. "Sorry." I had a flash of thirst at the sight of the red sparkling on Jack's fingertips, and the coppery tang of blood in the air. "They have a mind of their own sometimes," I slurred around the fangs that refused to retract.

Jack laughed and sat back. "I know what that's like." He ran a hand along the length of himself, and I shuddered as his fingers brushed my stomach. He shifted back off my hips, and I spread my legs to allow Jack access. His cock rested against the folds of my labia, and he ground himself against me. I cried out in pleasure as his throbbing cock brushed my clit and Jack grinned, moving faster and bringing another cry from me.

"Do you have a condom?" I suddenly realized as Jack slowed and grabbed his cock.

Jack gave me a patient look. "You're a vampire. You can't get STDs, or get pregnant."

"Oh, okay."

"Lube?" he asked in response.

"I, uh, I'm pretty wet already. I think we'll be fine."

"Oh, that hole!" Jack said with a laugh. I smiled along with him as he pushed the length of himself into me.

I gasped as Jack grabbed my legs and began rocking quicker inside me, getting deeper with each thrust until his balls were slapping my butt. His slick length rubbing me sent waves of pleasure shuddering through me.

"See that large bump at the top there?" Jack nodded.

"Rub it while you fuck me."

Jack moaned, lowering a hand to rub while he thrust. "It's so big," he said, twirling my clit between his fingers. I bit back a scream of ecstasy and gripped the bedsheets, bucking against Jack's hips as he rubbed. "Now it's my turn to say that your downstairs doesn't quite look like the straight porn I've seen," he said with a wry smile.

"Testosterone," I managed as pleasure overcame me. "Makes it grow." Jack let go of me and slid his hands under my butt to pull me closer. His firm chest pressed against my face as I sat up, reaching up to twine the fingers of my good hand through his hair.

I screamed in pleasure, bucking against Jack as I came.

Jack laughed and held me down. "Like fucking a tiger." He finished with a groan as he came inside me. Jack shuddered along with me for a moment before collapsing, leaning down to kiss me hard with his soft cock still inside me. We lay like that for a long moment. Jack was panting, but I didn't feel out of breath at all.

"That was wonderful," Jack said, recovering. He pulled out and rolled over to spoon me from behind.

"It was," I whispered, already feeling sleepy as the last of the aftershocks came over me with a last spasm of pleasure. I fell asleep, safe in Jack's arms.

CHAPTER 20

BETRAYED

I WOKE UP A few hours before dawn to an empty bed. I'd expected as much, but I still wished I could have woken to Jack's warmth next to me. Everything sounded quiet upstairs. I found a pile of new clothes waiting for me on the coffee table, along with a note from Jack.

> My fierce tiger,
>
> Sorry to sneak out on you like this, I have to go out for a few hours. There's some blood in the dumbwaiter for you. Call me if you need anything before I get back.
> Hugs and kisses.
>
> Love you,
>
> Jack

I smiled as I read it, and tucked it into my pocket to save it to read again later.

While I waited for the sun to go down, I took a shower, changed into the new clothes, and chugged down the breakfast of cold blood. One of these days I'd need to try adding it to coffee or something. Couldn't make it any worse-tasting that was for sure.

Since sunset was still over an hour away, I picked out a thriller novel off one of the shelves and sat down on the couch. I'd heard it was good, or at least good enough to have a movie made based on it, which I hadn't seen either.

The tablet was upstairs, and after what I saw on the news the other night, I was swearing off TV for a bit. So instead I lost myself in a fictional world of murder that, while ridiculous, was more believable than my current circumstances.

A door slammed upstairs, and then the floor creaked as if many people were walking around up there. I frowned and looked up at the clock on the wall. 11:00 pm. I'd gotten more caught up reading than I'd meant to; the book was as good as advertised. I wondered where Jack had been until so late. I hoped too that he hadn't gotten too much flak from Emily when he'd returned her car.

The door to the basement opened and then Jack's voice wafted down. "Everett, can you come upstairs please?" "Coming," I called, and put down the book.

When I got to the stairs, the door leading to the kitchen was open and no one was visible. I made my way up slowly, unable to help but feel like something was wrong.

Jack stood in the archway that led to the living room when I entered the kitchen. Waving me over, he smiled at me, but it didn't reach his eyes.

I hesitated and tilted my head, trying to see past Jack into the living room. "What's wrong?"

"Nothing's wrong." Jack's smile slipped. "We have some visitors with some good news." He stepped back into the living room and gestured for me to join him.

I wanted to ask why, if it was good news, Jack looked like he was attending a funeral, but instead I walked over to stand next to him in the archway. As I took in the crowd of visitors, Jack draped his arm over my shoulders, careful not to jostle my hurt shoulder. I recognized Stacy and one of the two men with her as Ted from the PCA. Besides them there were two more people, one man and one woman who I didn't know. All vampires if I had to guess, since they were with Stacy and Ted. I'd bet their presence was also the reason for Jack's bad mood.

"Good news," Stacy said. "The council has looked at your case and come to a decision. You're to be given this decade's slot."

She paused and looked at me expectantly, waiting for a reaction. Puzzled, I twisted my head to look up at Jack, who looked as baffled as I felt.

"Slot?" I asked, looking back at Stacy and then around the room. The female vampire's face twisted up in a snarl and she glared at me, but didn't say anything. Both men were impassive. "How is that the good news?"

Stacy sighed. "I suppose you don't know. In order to keep the vampire population in check so that there aren't more vampires in a given area than the human population can support, only a limited number of humans are allowed to be turned each decade."

I stared at her. "Wait, so what if a vampire is made without a slot, as you called it?"

"They are destroyed," Stacy said in a deadpan.

I blanched, and Jack's hand tightened on my uninjured arm.

"Don't worry." Stacy smiled and folded her hands in front of her. "You're getting the next slot, so you don't have to be destroyed."

"But I didn't have a choice!" I tried not to yell. I wasn't mad at her, but I couldn't help but be a little frustrated.

"Which is why the council ruled in your favor," Stacy said, her tone turning hard. The woman with her began grinding her teeth until Stacy shot her a hard look.

I took a deep breath, trying to calm myself. "And the other problem?"

"The council accepted Jack's proposed solution." Stacy smiled, as if that answered everything.

I glanced up at Jack. "And that is?"

"He didn't tell you?"

Jack had the grace to look embarrassed. "No. I didn't know if the council would agree, and there was no need to upset him unduly if there wasn't a need to," Jack said to Stacy, not meeting my eyes.

"Yes, the possessiveness you mentioned." Stacy gestured to the vampires flanking her. "That is why I brought backup. Ted, Luke, if you please."

I opened my mouth, but before I could say anything, the men darted forward and ripped me away from Jack's side. They twisted me around and threw me against the wall next to the door face-first, one holding each of my arms painfully behind my back. I cried out as my injured shoulder was ground into the wall.

"Hey, careful!" Jack yelled.

"He's just being dramatic," Stacy said. I couldn't see anything but plaster and vampire arm as my face was pressed against the wall. "Now, where does he keep it?"

Jack sighed. "Let me."

"Too dangerous," Stacy said. "You stay back."

"Look, he trusts me. And it's not like he isn't dangerous to you either." Jack's voice was patient.

"What?" the vampire holding my right arm asked. "What does he mean by that?"

Stacy sighed. "I wish you hadn't said anything, Jack."

"They'd have to find out eventually, Stacy. Just tell them to let him go."

"Fine, let him up."

The pressure on my arms disappeared and the men let me go, although they stayed where they were. I straightened my shirt and turned, feeling a bit boxed in by the much taller men on either side of me.

"We would have found out what?" the same vampire—now on my left—asked, giving me a wary look. "What danger is he to us? He's tiny."

I folded my arms and glared up at him. Luke by process of elimination, since I recognized Ted on my right.

"He's of a rare bloodline that can feed off other vampires," Stacy said, placing her hands on her cocked hips as she regarded me. The vampires on either side of me both sidled away a step away. "That line was thought to be extinguished thousands of years ago. No doubt part of the other reason the council let him live. Though other than the council telling me that, and that he is to be allowed to live, they wouldn't divulge any more details."

"On that note, any progress on finding my maker?" I asked, dropping my challenging gaze from Luke next to me to look at Stacy. I was genuinely curious, despite my anger at being ganged up on.

"No, but don't worry, we will." Stacy snapped her fingers and Jack moved over to stand in front of me, holding up a cloth bag. "The amulet. Now."

I glanced down at the bag and then around the room, finally getting the plan. "Wait, you're going to give a human mob boss a magical amulet? Jack did tell you what I found out about it, right?"

Stacy rolled her eyes. "She's only a human; she won't know what it does. We did some research on her. Her house is filled with stolen occult artifacts from around the world. No doubt she just wants it for her collection." Stacy waved a hand dismissively. "In a few months after your faked death, we'll send someone to steal it back, so she won't connect the theft to you."

Jack gave me a pleading look. "It's the fastest way to get her to call off her goons. I made contact with her today—"

"You what!" I jumped. "How? Why?"

"I was getting there." Jack gave me a patient look. "I called my old cell phone, she answered. I negotiated with her. The amulet for your life." He shook the bag. "So please, Everett, can you give it to me?"

I swallowed and licked my lips, but did as Jack asked and reached into my pocket. I pulled the amulet out and lifted it up to eye level to stare at it. I held it out over the bag and tried to drop it, but my fingers wouldn't let go. Someone moved in my peripheral vision. I snapped my arm back to my chest, crouched, and hissed at a startled-looking Jack. "No! It's mine! I won't let you steal it!"

Stacy pushed Jack aside as I lunged for him. Jack fell to the floor and Stacy caught me by the throat, holding me at arm's length. Luke and Ted grabbed my arms, and together the three shoved me to the floor and pinned me down. The woman rushed forward and tackled my flailing legs.

"Don't touch the gold with bare skin," Stacy called over the melee as they struggled to contain me in my frenzy. "We don't know what its effects might be."

I barely heard them over the voice in my head screaming at me to get away before they took my precious amulet.

Take it away and keep it safe.

After a few moments they managed to get me firmly pinned down, although it took the combined strength of four of them to keep me down. I was dimly aware of Jack nearby, but the voice beat at my mind, driving away any other thought except the amulet.

"Don't hurt him!" Jack yelled over the chaos. "And I need the amulet now if Zoe and I are going to make the meeting with Lady Ann in time."

"Lin, the muzzle," Stacy requested in a calm voice, as if she were sitting at a desk asking for a pencil rather than fighting a snapping, snarling vampire.

The woman sitting on my legs who been shooting me daggers earlier pulled out a leather face mask that looked like it had come right out of Silence of the Lambs, and tossed it to Stacy. She put it over my face, strapping it around the back of my head so tightly, the straps dug into my skin.

"Shit," Stacy said, letting go of my throat and standing up. I was still snapping at the vampires holding me. "We're going to have to sedate him."

"Ya think?" Ted gasped, barely keeping hold of my injured arm. Vaguely I knew it hurt to fight, but it was like the pain belonged to someone else.

Stacy came back, holding a needle filled with dark red fluid. She knelt and grabbed my hair, wrenching my head to the side, then plunged the needle into my neck. The world went black.

I WOKE UP WITH a pounding headache, and the feel of leather straps digging into my head. Something plastic-y yet pliable was wrapped around my entire body. I was so thirsty. I opened my eyes, but darkness greeted me.

Rock music blared from somewhere behind my head, almost drowning out the sound of two people conversing and the background hum of road noise. I recognized Stacy's voice, and thought the man talking to her might have been Ted. The surface I lay on bounced as the car went over a pothole.

All I could think of was the amulet. I could feel it moving away from me, and I wanted to scream in frustration. The voice was a little quieter now, giving me enough presence of mind to swallow the sound down to a low growl. Still, it was like someone else talked over my thoughts, making it hard for me to focus.

Jack was in danger, I could feel it. Lady Ann wasn't going to let things go that easily, but the voice in my head screaming about getting its amulet back quickly pushed all thoughts of Jack away.

It took me a few moments of wriggling to get my hands up from where the tight plastic had them pinned to my side. I grasped the material in front of my face and pulled until I had torn a large enough hole for me to see through. Sticking my arms through first, I got my head and shoulders out so I could sit up and look around. I was in a long car, lying on a gurney. A dark curtain hid the car's front seat. Thick straps circled my legs and torso—so that was why it'd been hard to move.

Wait, was I in a body bag? And was this a hearse? I shook my head. So cliché, vampires driving a hearse.

I fumbled with the buckles of the face mask, ripping it off with a satisfied grunt and tossing it away.

"What was that?" Stacy suddenly asked from the front seat. I twisted around to look behind me. A hand came through the curtain, pushing it aside to reveal Stacy's face. Her mouth dropped open as we locked eyes. She looked delicious. All I could see her as was a meal, although vaguely in the back of my mind I knew she had a name. My fangs descended, and I began fighting to pull my legs out of the bag.

"Fuck, Ted, he's awake! Pull over, pull over and come help me!" Stacy screamed, unbuckling her seat belt to begin climbing into the back seat.

"What the hell!" Ted yelled. "He should be out until at least tomorrow!"

The car abruptly slowed and jerked to the side, sending me and the gurney tumbling over. The gurney landed on top of me, but I didn't even feel it. I kicked my legs free and lunged for Stacy. My front half collided with her as she finished crawling into the back, slamming us both against the back of the front seats. I opened my mouth wide and bit her shoulder through her blouse. I sucked greedily at her blood. Stacy screamed and fought under me for only a moment before going limp from my venom.

The voice screamed at me to kill the one who took the amulet from me, but the blood hitting my stomach gave me a shock of clarity. The only thing I could compare it to was like when I'd had coffee the morning after a late night at the bar, and the caffeine hit. I let go, shoving the limp Stacy away from me while licking the last of her blood from my lips.

At that moment, Ted threw open the curtain and froze, eyes flicking back and forth between Stacy's motionless body and me. I grinned at him, showing off my fangs and bloody lips.

Ted pursed his lips and reached down slowly to unclip his seatbelt while our eyes remained locked. Before I could move, Ted had the door open and slid out. I lunged after him, but got tangled in the curtain. By the time I tore free of the fabric, Ted stood warily in front of the car.

I ignored him and climbed into the driver's seat, closing the car door. The keys still dangled from the ignition. Perfect. I started the hearse back up. Ted frowned, but backed over to the side of the road.

My feet couldn't even reach the pedals, so I adjusted the driver's seat closer to the steering wheel before putting the car into drive and flipping an abrupt U-turn. I ignored the angry honks of the other driver's and sped towards the amulet's pull. In the rearview mirror, I glanced back to see Ted standing where I'd left him. He had a cellphone pressed to his ear and was shouting at the person on the other end, gesturing at the retreating hearse.

In the back of the vehicle, Stacy slurred like a drunk, but I ignored her. I needed to get the amulet back. My amulet. The voice told me so. I'd feel better once I had it back. I didn't know where Jack was meeting Lady Ann, forcing me to drive back and forth through the streets as I tried to home in on its location. I followed the feeling north and west, and ended up on Lombard street going north past the industrial parks north of Saint John's, which were all dark and shuttered at this late hour.

I was getting close, I could feel it. The voice began to quiet as I drew nearer, letting me think more clearly.

"Jack, have to rescue Jack. Not the amulet. Jack," I said out loud in an attempt to remember why I was really here. I didn't care about the amulet, despite what the voice in my head was yelling. Let Lady Ann have it. But Jack, I had to protect Jack from her. She wasn't about to let my defiance of her go so easily, despite what she'd told him. She had to have figured out that Jack had been helping me, and she was going to punish him for it, I could feel it.

The clock on the dash said 12:48 am as the hearse bumped over the bridge over the Columbia Slough, where Lombard turned into Marine Drive. Suddenly, the amulet felt like it was behind me.

The voice screamed so loud in my head that I felt like a spear was being stabbed through my face. My vision went black. I took my foot off the gas and my hands off the steering wheel to clutch my aching head. The car swerved to the right, bouncing onto the sidewalk before hitting a streetlight with a crash.

The airbags went off with a bang, smacking me in the face. In the back, Stacy cried out as she was flung halfway into the front seat. Her eyes were still glazed over and she lay there moaning, covered in broken glass from the shattered windshield. Steam rose from the engine where it was wrapped around the light pole.

"Amulet, amulet, amulet!" the voice screamed in my head. Or maybe it was me screaming out loud. "Back, back, go, fast. Ours."

I kicked the bent driver's-side door and stumbled out clutching my aching head.

"No, Jack. Jack."

It was like my thoughts were fighting, pulling me in two. But my mind was united on one thing: I needed to go, now, towards the amulet. Where Jack would be.

I took off running down the road leading north, past the Kelley Point Park sign. The yellow gate that would have normally be closed at this late hour was wide open.

Kelley Point Park wasn't a bad place for an exchange that you wanted to keep as quiet as possible. The heavily forested park lay on the little strip of land between where the Willamette River split from the Columbia, and was surrounded by business and industrial parks that were empty at night. There were no residential areas anywhere nearby.

Behind me, metal squealed as Stacy crawled out of the car. I glanced over my shoulder to see her swaying on her feet, clutching the side of the wrecked hearse to stay upright. She called out in a slurred voice, "Everett, Jack didn't go alone! Come back! Nothing's going to happen to him! Zoe's with him."

I ignored her and kept running.

CHAPTER 21

THE RITUAL

I FOUND EMILY'S WHITE sedan—the bullet holes down the side from our wild flight out of Mount Hood made it pretty clear it was her car—in the parking lot along with half-a-dozen others, but no one was around. I wondered why Jack was still driving it, but that was a question for later.

I could tell I was close to the amulet now, because the voice in my head had begun to calm down. Now I could hear it only if I stopped and concentrated. It made me half wonder if the new voice had been there the whole time since I'd become a vampire, but I didn't have time to ponder it right now.

A man—a human wearing a black suit and tie with a transparent earpiece over one ear—stepped out from between two of the cars. I tackled him, burying my fangs in his neck before he managed to cry out. For a few moments he flailed against my admittedly light weight on his back, but then he began to relax, sinking slowly down to the pavement. I drank eagerly and deeply for a few moments before pulling away. I didn't want to kill the guy, only incapacitate him. He sprawled on the pavement, still breathing, but eyes glazed and groaning.

Feeling much better, I stood and looked around the parking lot, trying to figure out where everyone was. Several paths led off from the parking lot, one heading west, one north, and one southwest. I could smell smoke and see a faint glimmer off through the trees to the north, so I headed that way. Rather than walk on the path and make myself a target, I walked parallel to it, using the trees' shadows as coverage. I probably should have been stealthy earlier coming into the park, but the voice screaming in my head had made thinking hard.

A ring of tiki torches came into view ahead. A woman in a business suit stood inside the circle, her back to me. She was talking to someone that I couldn't see, in a voice too low for me to make out the words from this distance. There were about a dozen people scattered around keeping watch, but they were only human, and I easily spotted them with my vampire night-vision.

I could smell blood in the air. Several of the human guards had visible bite marks and torn clothing. The bites looked like dog bites. Or maybe jackal bites, I realized through the fogginess of my thoughts. I hoped Jack had fought his way free from this trap and was now somewhere safe.

Moving slowly, I circled around to avoid the two guards watching the path. My new position also gave me a better angle into the circle, but what I saw made my heart sink. He hadn't gotten away after all. Jack and Zoe were being held by two black-suited security guards each. Handcuffs around Jack's and Zoe's wrists glinted in the torchlight. Jack looked pissed, and only because I'd spent so much time with him over the last few days was I able to tell how scared he was.

Now that I could see the business-suited woman's face, I recognized Lady Ann from Kevin's memory.

Lady Ann lifted a bowl up above her head and began chanting in a guttural language that I didn't recognize. Meanwhile, the two guards on Zoe forced her to her knees, and the two holding Jack dragged him backwards out of the circle. Jack yelled and fought them, but with his cuffed wrists— and bound legs too I saw now—they had him overpowered. When Jack planted his feet and refused to move, one guard grabbed Jack's hands, the other his feet, and they carried him away—dangling between them like he weighed no more than his clothing—and dropped him outside the circle.

"Change," I hissed under my breath. "Jack, change and run away." Why didn't Zoe or Jack change? I prayed they did something, anything. Keeping supernaturals secret from humans was important, but at some point you had to just say screw it and opt for self-preservation.

The amulet was close, I could feel it, but I didn't see it anywhere. With this many guards about, and the threat that they too were armed with silver-laced bullets like Lady Ann's thugs last night, I didn't dare make a move until I was sure where my target was. As I'd learned last night, my speed only helped so much. I needed to get the amulet back before I could help Jack. Not that I didn't care about Jack more than the amulet, but if the voice screamed at me again while I was running away with

Jack—and I knew it would if I got farther away from the amulet again—I'd probably collapse and then we'd both be caught, which wouldn't improve either of our situations.

Something on the ground at Lady Ann's feet glinted in the firelight. I tensed, ready to run, before I registered that it was silver and not gold.

Lady Ann finished chanting while I scanned for a sign, any sign, of where the amulet might be. I saw the bag Jack'd been asking me to put the amulet in earlier discarded on the grass between the circle and the trees, but from the flatness of the folds it was clearly empty.

Where could the amulet be? Lady Ann's sleek suit didn't show any bulges, and probably didn't even have any pockets anyway. I was unfortunately all too familiar with women's clothing and its pockets or lack thereof.

Did one of the guards have it? I closed my eyes and turned my head, trying to judge direction, opening my eyes when it felt like it was directly in front of me, only to find myself staring right at Lady Ann. I snuck a few dozen more feet in the trees around the circle of torches, only for the same thing to happen again. So where was she keeping it?

Lady Ann's chanting slowed to a stop. She lowered the bowl and knelt to place it in the dirt directly in front of the kneeling Zoe. The guards forced Zoe to lean over, head down over the bowl. Lady Ann reached to her side and picked up the glinting silver object I'd noticed earlier, revealing it to be a large knife. With her other hand she grabbed Zoe's hair. Zoe fought and bucked, but with Lady Ann holding her head steady and the two men restraining her arms, she couldn't move.

Lady Ann yelled another line in the same language as the chanting, and before I realized what was happening, ran the knife along Zoe's throat. Blood poured out of the gaping slash on her neck into the gold bowl. It was so much blood.

I was both horrified by and drawn to the gush of red liquid. I covered my mouth, but my fangs were already down and pressing into my lips. If I hadn't drunk from Stacy and the guard earlier, I wouldn't have been able to keep myself from rushing forward. As it was, I struggled to not burst out of the brush and reveal myself.

Jack screamed wordlessly, fighting against the grips of the two men restraining him. Why didn't he change and run?

Zoe twitched for what felt like too long. Finally she stopped moving and her eyes glazed over in death, although blood continued to drip from her throat for several long minutes. When it stopped, Lady Ann let go of her hair and the two guards dragged Zoe's limp body back and dropped it on the dirt. She landed on her side, her dead eyes staring accusingly right at me still hidden in the trees. For a moment her face merged with Lindsay's in my memory, even though aside from the dead eyes and the slashed throat, they looked nothing alike.

Lady Ann reached into the gold bowl, and when she pulled her hand back out, it was clean. Odd. That bowl had been catching all of Zoe's blood; Lady Ann's hand should have been coated in it. She stood and unbuttoned the top two buttons of her shirt, then pressed something against her chest, flattening it palm down.

"With this heart's blood," Lady Ann said in English, but in a ritualistic cadence and tone, "I invoke thee."

She stood there for a long moment. The only sound came from the crackling of the flames in the tiki torches. She pulled her hand from her chest and looked down at her palm with a petulant frown. "That's odd. I don't feel any different."

Her hand tilted, and I finally saw what she was holding: my amulet. The voice in my head crowed with delight, urging me to run and take what was mine. I shook with the effort of not moving. Even moving fast, I wouldn't be able to take the amulet from her and protect Jack.

Jack sobbed. "Zoe. You killed her."

Lady Ann's head snapped up and she narrowed her eyes at Jack. "Perhaps it needs a male..." she muttered low. Then she raised her voice and pointed at the men holding Jack. "Bring him over here and let's try this again."

"Jack!" Before I realized what I was doing I burst from the trees, running with my vampire speed. "No!" I yelled as I dashed for Jack. I had eyes only for him, so the crack of a gun caught me by surprise. The force of the bullet smashing into my left leg sent me crashing to the ground, and I screamed in surprise as much as in pain.

The momentum sent me tumbling and rolling across the dirt for several feet before I came to a stop, clutching my leg. It burned like silver.

"Everett!" Jack yelled, lunging forward only to be caught by the guards.

"You!" Lady Ann growled, glaring at me. "What did you do to my amulet? It worked for you, so why not me?"

"I don't know what you're talking about," I gasped, clawing at my pant leg. I ripped it open to reveal a bullet hole in my upper thigh. Black lines were quickly spreading out from the wound.

"Goddamnit, Everett!" Jack yelled, struggling against the guards. "You were supposed to stay away, where it was safe!"

"I wasn't about to let her hurt you!" I snarled back around my fangs. It was getting easier to talk with them. "Why didn't you change and run?"

Lady Ann smirked. "He can't. I know all about your little werecoyote friend, Everett."

"Jackal," Jack and I said at the same time.

"Whatever." She waved a hand dismissively as she paraded across the dirt towards me, walking like she was strutting down a catwalk and not across a muddy clearing. When she reached the torches, she fingered some purple flowers that had been twined around all the poles. I hadn't paid them any mind, thinking they were just decorations for the ritual. "Wolfsbane."

"So?" I struggled to pay attention to her words. The pain in my leg was growing worse and I couldn't get my fangs to retract.

Lady Ann put a hand on her hip and pivoted to regard the dead body of Zoe, and then glanced at Jack. "Prevents shapeshifters from changing. At least that was how the legends went. Glad to see more than one legend got things right."

She turned and stalked over to me. When she got to me, she placed a foot on my bullet wound and ground her heel into it. I screamed at the pain, and lunged for her leg with my teeth. A wooden baseball bat cracked me across the cheek, jerking my head to the side. Someone grabbed me from behind and stuffed whole cloves of garlic in my mouth, followed by a thick leather strap which they tied behind my head.

The smell and taste of the garlic made me retch and choke, but the gag kept me from spitting them out. I reached up to claw the gag loose, but the same guard snapped a metal handcuff around my wrist and then locked my hands behind me. Then rough hands grabbed my elbows and pulled me to my feet. My injured leg wouldn't hold my weight, and I would have collapsed except for the man behind me holding me upright.

"Hmm, the garlic one seems to have some merit too." She sniffed. "Pity. I love Italian food. Ah, well."

A guard smashed a balloon into the top of my head. It exploded, spraying water everywhere. Water cascaded down my hair and dripped from my nose. I shook my head to get the worst of it off me.

"Holy water has no apparent affect," Lady Ann said. "Interesting. Well, I'd love to experiment on you all night, but we're on a tight deadline. Take him into the circle. He'll be the next sacrifice to the ancient one."

"No, you promised!" Jack pleaded as the guard shoved me forward. My shot leg wouldn't hold my weight, and I collapsed. I tried to catch myself, but with my hands bound I landed on my face in the dirt. I rolled to the side before the thug lifted me back up by one arm.

"What?" Lady Ann said, crossing her hands under her bosom.

"Everett's life for the amulet," Jack said, straightening to look her in the eye. "Let him go. I'll be your willing sacrifice. Perhaps that is what went wrong with your first ritual."

"Hmm..." She shifted and tapped a finger on her chin. "You might be right at that. And I did promise. Agreed then."

"No!" I tried to yell around the gag and the garlic without success.

Jack shot me a pleading look. "Uncuff him first. Let him go, to prove your good faith."

As if I would just leave Jack here to die. I shook my head, glaring right back at Jack on the other side of the circle.

Lady Ann shook her head, a smile tugging at her lips. "I can tell by the look on his face that he'd not be inclined to leave well enough alone. Be confident that if your death completes the ritual that I will have gotten what I wanted and will be happy to let him go."

"And if it fails?" Jack glanced at Zoe's cooling body. "Again?"

Lady Ann shrugged. "Then I suppose you'll get to be together in the afterlife. Let's be clear here, I hold all the cards. At least one of you will die tonight, no matter what you do."

"How many people are you willing to throw into the meat grinder over whatever it is you are trying to accomplish?" Jack stood tall and regal despite the guards holding his arms. I would have swooned over him if I weren't choking on garlic with my leg screaming in agony. "What are you trying to accomplish here, anyway?"

"As many as it takes," Lady Ann snapped back and glanced at the watch on her wrist. "I'm dying. Aggressive brain cancer. Inoperable. All my money and power can do nothing for me. Chemotherapy didn't work. There is no cure. At least, none known to medicine. When modern science failed me, I turned my gaze elsewhere." She paused and her eyes grew distant.

She held my amulet out and turned it over in her hand, admiring it. "Took me over six months to track this down after I became aware of it from one of my new friends, who said this amulet might have the cure I was searching for. The last recorded mention of it was from a Victorian archaeologist's notes. However, it was stolen somewhere between the dig site and England. Lost to the black market. Imagine my surprise when my private investigator discovered it in the background of a picture taken right here in Portland in the 1910's. The old fool hadn't even known what he had. Neither did the museum he donated it to, which is where you came in." Her face turned hard and she turned her head to glare at me. "You almost ruined everything."

"You just want to become a vampire?" Jack shook his head, eyes wide.

"You think that's what he is?" She gestured at me while turning back to Jack. "No, he's something more. I don't want to spend my life hiding in shadows, like these weak, modern things that call themselves vampires. If I'm going to live forever, I want to do it in power and style, like the old ones. This amulet is the key to bringing them back, to make things like they were in the ancient times, where monsters ruled and it was the humans cowering in their houses at night." She glanced at her watch again. "I've said too much, and the night won't last forever. Decide now. Nobly sacrifice yourself for your boyfriend, or watch him die. Your choice."

Jack glanced at me again, and his mouth flattened out into a line. "Sacrifice. I'll be your sacrifice."

I wanted to scream, "Who's being selfish now!" but with the gag and garlic, all that came out was a muffled cry.

"Excellent." Lady Ann gestured. "You there, as a show of good faith, take off his leg restraints. Let him walk in under his own power, to prove his commitment."

One of the guards pulled a set of keys from his pocket and knelt down to unlock the cuffs on Jack's legs, while Lady Ann walked back into the circle and dropped my amulet back into the bowl. Of course, that was why Zoe's blood had disappeared; the amulet had sucked it into itself. The voice in my head was ranting about the amulet, but it was getting easier to ignore it now that I could distinguish it from my own thoughts.

"Kneel in front of me," Lady Ann ordered, laying the knife back into place at her feet and picking up the bowl.

I jerked and twisted, horrified as Jack walked forward and dropped down onto the grass in front of her. Lady Ann lifted the bowl above her head and began repeating the same chanting ritual she'd done before killing Zoe. Jack glanced at me with a resigned look.

I saw red. The voice whispered to me how to break the handcuffs and kill the guard on me. I gave in. I had to save Jack.

Listening to the voice's whispered instructions, I broke the handcuffs with a quick twist of my wrists. The guard holding me up by my arms barely had time to give a gasp of disbelief before I tensed my legs and jumped up, snapping my head back into his face. He staggered backwards with a pained grunt, blood spraying from his broken nose.

I ripped the gag off with both hands, easily snapping the thick leather, and spat out garlic bulbs as soon as it tore free. I swallowed a few in my haste, making me feel a little sick, but I swallowed hard and kept moving.

Kill him, the voice whispered. I listened. I turned and pounced on the falling guard, teeth wrapping around his throat before he even hit the ground. Out of the corner of my eye I saw the other suited men drawing guns. I didn't have much time.

Rather than sucking, I bit down hard and jerked my head up, ripping the entire front of the man's throat out. Arterial blood geysered up from the wound, coating me from head to toe.

Spitting the chunk of meat out, I took a few gulps from the spray before using vampire speed to run at the nearest guard. The man was still lifting his gun to sight on me when I reached him. I smacked the gun to the side with one hand while backhanding his face with the other to expose his throat. Teeth bared, I lunged. I ripped and tore more than sucked, only getting a few mouthfuls of blood before the man crumpled, like a puppet with its strings cut.

A gunshot barked suddenly in the silence. Pain blossomed up my arm, and the impact whirled me around. It hurt, but distantly. The voice pushed me on. I caught my balance and then sprinted at the gunner, who widened her eyes, finger tightening on the trigger again. I reached her and smacked the gun away right before it went off. The bullet swung wide, hitting a tree and sending chips of bark flying. I grabbed the woman's head and tackled her to the ground, using my momentum to twist her head sharply to the side as we fell together. The crack of the woman's neck snapping was almost as loud as the gunshots had been.

Lady Ann continued chanting, though her face was twisted in a snarl and her voice turned harsh. She sped up the tempo of her chant. I had to hurry, but the three guards on the other side of the tiki torch circle had drawn their guns and were sighting on me. I had to take care of them before going after Lady Ann, or their silver-coated bullets would kill me before I'd be able to finish her.

I grabbed the dead woman and lifted her body in front of me like a shield as I got up. Three more gunshots boomed, and her lifeless body jerked as they hit. I ran around the circle at regular human speed, limping harshly on my injured leg. I was tiring.

Although I'd fed well off Stacy and the first guard I'd run into, I'd been shot twice now with silver bullets and had been heavily using my vampire speed. I licked the blood off my lips as I ran, but I needed more. Another bullet struck the dead woman, but I was close enough to the shooters now that it went through and hit me in the chest. I gasped. Even slowed down by going through her dead flesh first, it still hurt.

I threw her body at the gunners as I limped forward. Their ducking away to avoid it bought me a few precious seconds.

I sped back up to vampire speed, despite my fatigue. The nearest man lifted his gun to aim at my head. I grabbed a torch as I sped towards him, propping it under my arm like a lance. The tip hit the man's chest just as he pulled the trigger. The shot went wide, but not wide enough, and the side of my head erupted in pain as the bullet grazed the side of my head. I dropped my makeshift lance and the impaled guard fell screaming to the ground, chest ablaze from the still-burning torch sticking from his chest. The oil had splattered over his clothes and the fire spread rapidly.

I ignored him, not slowing down as I continued around the circle. The next guard's eyes were wide, and his arms and hands shook with panic as he aimed at me. His gun cracked, and the dirt to my left erupted. I ducked down under his outstretched arms and punched him in the throat. The guard dropped his gun and fell, clutching at his neck and gasping for air.

Another woman and man stepped out of the treeline, raising guns at me. Shit. I didn't have time for this.

The cadence of Lady Ann's chanting changed, and I risked a glance back to see her lowering the bowl. I'd have hoped that Jack would take advantage of my distraction to run since his legs were now unbound, but he was still calmly kneeling in front of her, his head held high and defiance in his eyes.

No time to take care of the new gunners; I had to get there before she slit his throat. I spun and ran back toward them, ignoring the newcomers. There was the crack of gunfire and a bullet struck my lower back. I was thrown forward, barely catching myself from falling face-first onto the grass. My legs refused to move.

There was a second shot, and Kevin screamed. "Everett, go! Run! I'll hold them off." His warning was followed by the rapid cracks of gunfire. I glanced over my shoulder to see the woman who'd entered the clearing with him dead at his feet, and Kevin gunning down another black-suited guard coming out of the woods. I didn't know why he was helping me, but I'd take all the help I could get.

The pain blossoming up from the gunshot wound in my back was enough to drown out the voice. For a moment I was back fully, my thoughts my own. So thirsty. It hurt. My fangs ached.

Two meals were directly in front of me, one kneeling down with his back to me. I let out a wordless cry, crawling toward my helpless prey's exposed back. The woman caught sight of me over the other's shoulder and smirked, lifting a knife toward my prey's neck. The man tipped his head back to expose his throat.

I didn't know why, but this sent a shudder of fury through me. With a last burst of strength, I lunged forward and shoved the man aside as the woman slashed sideways with the knife. The blade caught me across the face, cutting deeply. Blood sprayed from my check, splattering the bowl.

Magic exploded out from the amulet with an earsplitting crack. The wave of power threw us all flying away in opposite directions. All the torches were ripped out of the ground with the force of the blast, and the nearest trees snapped in half with loud cracks.

I landed half on top of the man I'd shoved out of the way. My prey. Warm blood pulsed under me. So close, separated from me only by a thin layer of skin. I inhaled deeply, savoring the intoxicating scent of the man's blood. The man's cheek had been struck by flying debris, and a thin trickle of blood welled from the cut. I crawled up the man to lick at the blood, shuddering with pleasure as each drop hit my tongue. The meal under me was frozen in fear, his heart hammering widely under my palms.

The voice in my head urged me to drink deeply, to revitalize myself, but I resisted. I opened my mouth and rested my fangs lightly on the man's neck. The pulse of the blood jumping against my lips was almost too much to bear. I wanted it, badly, yet was not sure why I held back.

A woman moaned behind me. I snapped my head up and around to focus on what had made the sound. Another meal was there. I could feel her warmth from here, and this one I didn't have any qualms about eating. I tried to stand, but my legs wouldn't move. I crawled toward her, growling low in my throat.

She opened her eyes as I reached her. She gasped and began crying, pushing herself back from me.

"No, no, don't eat me!" she sobbed between shuddering tears. "I'll give you anything you want. Money. Fame. Just spare me. Or, or," Lady Ann pleaded, eyes glinting through her tears, "yes, turn me to be like you."

Her words were meaningless. I grabbed her leg with my good hand, pulling her toward me. She screamed and twisted onto her belly to claw at the dirt, trying to get away, but she was only human. When she was close enough, I grabbed her hair and pulled her head to me, pushing her chin back to bury my mouth against her neck. I carefully pierced her artery with my fangs and sucked deeply, taking my time, making sure not to waste a single drop.

At first, she batted at my head with her fists, but after a few moments, she relaxed limply under me. I kept sucking until her heart stopped beating, and then lay there for a long moment, licking up the last few drops that welled out. When the blood stopped flowing, I pushed her away and looked around for the amulet.

It had been thrown by the blast, but I could feel it in my head when I concentrated, and it didn't take me long to home in on it. I crawled toward it and snatched it up, petting it with reverence as I stared at it.

I don't know how long I stared at it, but suddenly Stacy was there, snapping her fingers in front of my face.

"Everett?"

I blinked at her and hissed, clutching the amulet to my chest. "Mine!"

"Yes, yours," Stacy said, giving me a motherly smile. "I won't try to take it. Do you know where you are?"

I blinked, trying to order my thoughts. Now that I was holding the amulet again, the voice was silent and I could think. Slowly events slotted themselves in place in my mind. "Oh, god. I almost ate Jack." My hands began to shake and I covered my mouth with my hands, pressing the amulet against my lips. It smelled of blood.

"But you didn't." Stacy gave me an encouraging smile. "He's fine."

I looked around finally, taking in what had changed. Stacy wasn't the only vampire present. Ted was there, along with the rest from the house.

But Jack was gone, as was Zoe's body.

"Jack?" I asked. "Where is he?" My voice raised in panic.

"He's fine," Stacy said reassuringly. "He's getting medical attention back by the cars. He told us what happened. Now, do you feel coherent enough to come with me?"

I lowered my hands and hugged myself. I shook my head. "Hurts. Thirsty. Don't want to..." I swallowed and shook my head harder. My whole body screamed in pain. My fangs and the back of my throat ached with thirst. "What happened? That blast?"

Stacy frowned. "We're not sure. It seems our research on the amulet has suddenly become more urgent." She gave me a hard look. "Would you like to be sedated?"

I gulped, and my grip on the amulet tightened. "Like what you did to me earlier? What if you take the amulet and I lose control again?"

"That's a valid concern, Everett, but I assure you, until we figure out what it is, we won't try to take the amulet from you again. That seemed to be the trigger, not the sedative."

"You're sure Jack's okay?" I let out a breath and met Stacy's eyes.

"I'm sure. Would you feel better if you talk to him on the phone?"

"No, I'm sure he doesn't want to hear from me. I almost..." I shook my head again, holding back tears. "No sedation. I'm in control, but I can't walk."

"Jack told us. They were using silver bullets." Stacy's concerned frown dropped away and her eyes narrowed. "We need to find that rogue vampire sooner rather than later. First turning a mortal without permission, and now telling another human how to hurt us."

"I'm not sure anyone told her," I said slowly, opening my hand to look at the amulet. "I think she was figuring it out as she went along. Like the garlic she stuffed in my mouth. It didn't hurt. I choked, sure, but—"

"Wait, garlic?" Stacy blinked at me in surprise, smoothing her skirt under her legs to kneel next to me. "Garlic doesn't hurt vampires. That's a myth. Actually, if you have humans rub garlic oil on their skin before you bite them, it gives the blood a pleasant taste."

"I think she was testing the myths. She said as much about the wolfsbane. She was experimenting."

"Odd." Stacy tapped a finger on her lips, her eyes growing distant.

"She said something else strange. She said the amulet worked for me, but not for her. Maybe there is no rogue vampire. Do you think," I held the amulet up between thumb and finger to show it to Stacy, "that this is what changed me?"

Stacy shook her head. "That would be unprecedented. And impossible, as far as I know."

I sighed and slipped it in my pocket. I almost mentioned the voice I'd been hearing to her, but hesitated. I probably sounded unhinged enough, and was on thin ice after everything I'd done so far: killing another vampire, drinking from Stacy, and wrecking their hearse. Plus this whole mess in the park.

Stacy patted my leg. "We'll figure it out later. In the meantime, we need to get you back to the house and get some blood in you."

"Where is Everett? Is he okay?" Kevin's voice wafted over to me, and I whipped my head around to look. The officer was being restrained by two vampires, who were dragging him away.

Ted came over to Stacy. "Sorry, ma'am. He slipped away from the guards."

"No, bring him over," I said. "He helped me earlier, I want to know why."

Ted frowned and looked at Stacy, who shrugged. "Why not?" she said.

The vampires holding Kevin let him go. He rushed forward and dropped to his knees in front of me. He looked me over critically, and then surprising leaned over and hugged me. I blinked in surprise, then gritted my teeth and pushed him away, trying to keep myself from burying my fangs in the oh-so-tempting neck so close to my mouth.

"What is going on?" I asked, trying not to breathe too deeply of Kevin's pleasant scent.

A smile tugged the corner of Stacy's mouth. "Are those fang marks?" she asked as Kevin sat back, smiling amiably at me.

"Yeah, I might have bit him yesterday. Why?" I asked, still puzzled. "Jack said that vampire venom makes people drunk, like alcohol, but that doesn't explain why he's looking at me now like a lost puppy dog."

"Vampire venom is also addictive. Hits some people harder than others." Stacy patted the grinning Kevin's leg. "Makes hunting easier when the prey wants to come back to you. Congratulations. You've got your first groupie."

EPILOGUE

Three weeks later...

I'D BEEN STAYING WITH some mages while recovering from the silver-laced gunshots. They had examined me and the amulet, and also questioned me, Kevin, and Jack about the ceremony. They were trying to piece together what her ceremony had been meant to accomplish. I'd told the vampires about the ancient book I'd seen in Kevin's memory, the one that Lady Ann had been consulting, but they hadn't been able to locate it.

The conclusion so far was that the amulet had been what turned me, although they weren't sure how yet. One thing that they had been able to determine was that the amulet was tied to my life force. So for now it stayed with me, hanging from a chain around my neck under my shirt.

There was a knock at the front door. I answered it, and found Jack standing on the front porch. He grinned as I stepped outside and pulled him into a hug. His arms tightened around me, pressing me against his chest. My backpack straps dug into my chest.

After a moment he loosened his arms and looked down at me. "Where's your binder? I didn't feel it."

I grinned and let go of him to step back. "So it turns out that being a vampire does have a few perks after all." I grabbed the bottom of my T-shirt and lifted it up to show Jack my perfect, scarless chest. "The vampire doctor that treated me for the gunshot wounds gave me top surgery."

Apparently vampires healed quickly and without scaring, but they couldn't regrow much tissue. If your arm got cut off and the severed arm was reunited with the stump it could be reattached, but if the arm got lost, you'd be spending the rest of eternity with only one hand. The good news for me was that it meant that after the doctor took out my breast tissue, it wouldn't regrow. And vampire healing left me without any visible scars.

"Wow, I'll say." Jack put a palm flat on my chest, running it down my bare skin before pulling his hand away with a sigh. "Wish we had time to properly enjoy it. Looks like you're ready to go?"

I nodded and dropped my shirt front to heft my backpack. "Let's roll."

"That really everything you own?" Jack asked as we went down the steps.

"Yeah. Since I was declared dead, I couldn't exactly go back home and pack up my things."

The vampires had used the incident at the park to fake my death. The official story was that I'd broken into the park to kill myself. I'd gotten cold feet and pulled the gun from my head at the last second. The gun had still gone off and the bullet struck a propane tank that had subsequently exploded, killing me.

Such a stupid way to go. It didn't make me feel any better that it was a lie.

We got to the street, and I stopped short at the sight of Emily's white sedan. The bullet holes had been badly patched, making it obvious he was still driving the same car.

I pointed to the car as Jack unlocked the car with the key fob. "Why are you still driving Emily's car?"

Jack got in without answering and I threw my bag in the backseat, then got in the front passenger seat. The cloth of the front seats still had red stains from our blood. I gave him another questioning look as I buckled my seatbelt.

Jack put the car in drive and pulled away from the curb before answering. "As you can imagine, she was a little pissed when I showed back up with her brand-new car shot up. I ended up agreeing to buy it from her so she could get another new car."

"I'm sorry." I winced. "At least it's still drivable."

"You mean unlike my other car that got shot up?" Jack let out an amused laugh, letting me know he wasn't mad.

I gave him a small smile. "I hope you blamed me for everything."

"Totally." Jack barked out another laugh.

I laughed with him for a moment before sobering. "Stacy said you went to my funeral."

Jack's expression hardened. "Yeah. Your parents are both alive and well. The rest... Are you sure you want to hear the rest?" We stopped at a red light and he turned to look at me. The red lit his face up eerily in the dark, and I shivered at the ominous look in his eyes.

"Yes. What was it like?"

Jack sighed, but the light turned green and he had to turn away from me to watch the road. "All the pictures they put out of you were pre-transition, and they only called you by your dead name with 'she' pronouns. Your mom recognized me from the Ren Faire when I tried to talk to her about getting your legal name on the tombstone, and she refused to talk to me. I'm sorry."

I'd been expecting something like that. I thought I'd be angry at having my worst fears confirmed, but instead I only felt resigned. I'd done my best to make up with them before my death and they'd pushed me away. It didn't matter now, anyway. That was now literally a different life.

Jack seemed to sense my conflicting thoughts and kept quiet, for which I was grateful. I watched the dark streets flash by out the window for the rest of the long drive to my home for the next little while.

The vampires' house for new blood, as it were, was out in the middle of nowhere southeast of Portland. PCA owned ten acres of land that the house sat in the middle of. A safe place for new vampires to learn to control themselves and their abilities.

Stacy had explained to me that new vampires lived together here for their first decade as a sort of probationary period, under the supervision of an elder mentor vampire. There were two other new ones living here at the moment, in addition to the mentor. The oldest was coming up on the end of her time here, and was in the process of moving out.

In the meantime, since there were only supposed to be two at any given time and all the current residents had refused to share a room with me even temporarily, I was going to be relegated to sleeping in a light-proofed box in the corner of the living room. A coffin. I was not looking forward to it.

I'd argued with Stacy that since I'd already proved I could control myself, I shouldn't be subject to the same restrictions as other new vampires. I'd lost. Stacy made it clear that I'd already been given enough exceptions to the rules by being allowed to live. Going through the introductory time out of society was mandatory for every new vampire, and that if I didn't submit I'd be destroyed, control or not.

Just my bad luck that Lin was the current house mentor. She'd applied for the position on the basis of her boyfriend being the next vampire turned, but now was stuck with me—which at least explained her antagonism to me when I'd met her at the safe house.

Jack turned off the highway, and we rolled down a very long driveway that wound its way through the woods. At the end we came to a stop in front of a big old two-story farmhouse, remarkable only in the fact that all the upper story windows were blacked out. The only light came from a flickering porchlight that only served to make the house even creepier looking.

"Last stop." Jack turned the car off and got out with me. While I stared up at the dark house, Jack got my backpack out and handed it to me.

"Don't go!" I dropped my bag onto the pavement and flung my arms around Jack's waist, bursting into tears. "Did Stacy tell you?"

Jack hugged be tightly. "That it'll be a year before you're allowed a phone? Yes. I'll miss you a lot, but you'll be fine. You're my fierce tiger, remember?"

I pulled away and stuck my tongue out at him. "I'm never going to live down that nickname, am I?"

"Not ever, Tiger." Jack laughed and ruffled my hair. I laughed with him, wiping away my tears.

The door to the house creaked open, spilling a square of brighter light out onto the porch. I recognized Lin's profile outlined in the doorway. She had her hands on her hips.

"Time to go," I said, leaning over to grab my bag.

"One last thing," Jack said, stepping between me and the house. "Will you be my boyfriend?"

"Yes." I grinned widely and got up on my tiptoes to give Jack a kiss.

"I'll be waiting for you!" Jack called after me as I made my way toward the house.

I sighed deeply, stopping as I got to the porch and turned to wave goodbye to him one last time.

This was going to be a long year.

BOOK 2: WHILE EVERETT struggles to learn how to be a vampire, Jack tracks down an elusive vampire killer moving across the globe towards Portland. A killer he thinks might be Everett's maker.

Bloodline of the Ancients is available at https://books2read.com/u/38yBZ7

BONUS CONCEPT ART

Art by Beleoci

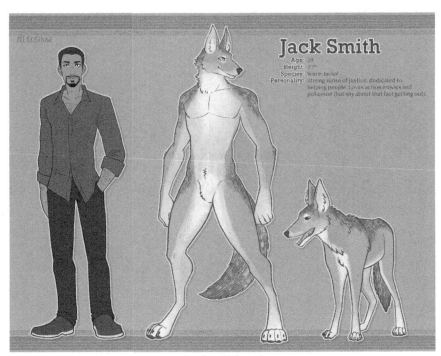

Art by Beleoci

The Amulet, front and back. Art by Lychgate

ALSO BY ROAN ROSSER

<u>The Changing Bodies Series</u>
Book 1 - Ritual of the Ancients - Coming May 13, 2022
Book 2 - Bloodline of the Ancients - Coming July 13, 2022
Book 3 - Goddess of the Ancients - Coming August 16, 2022
Prequel - Jackal of Hearts – Newsletter Freebie
<u>The Chaos Menagerie Series</u>
Book 1 - Red Pandamonium - Coming June 13, 2022
Book 1.5 - Diamond in the Rat – Newsletter Freebie
Book 2 – Pandora's Fox – Coming Soon

About the Author

ROAN ROSSER

My urban fantasy novels mainly feature the trans and queer protagonists grappling with things like identity and found families that I wished I could have read about growing up.

I escaped from the bowels of Utah (namely Provo) and now live in the sunny Pacific Northwest of the United States.

When not writing, you can probably find me beating up pixel baddies or in front of one of my sewing machines adding to my overstuffed closet or my army of homemade plush dolls.

If you find yourself blinded by the vivid colors and loud patterns of my homemade shirts, know that I'm only trying to warn you that I may be poisonous. Or venomous? Or both? Probably both.